THE DAY THE WORLD SNEEZED

MARCH 12, 2020

THE DAY THE WORLD SNEEZED
BY EDDIE JONES
Dry Bones Publishing

ISBN: 9781938499364

Available in print from your local bookstore and online booksellers.

For more information on this book and the author visit: EddieJones.org

This is a work of fiction. Names, characters, and incidents are all products of the author's warped imagination or are used for fictional purposes. Any mentioned brand names, places, and trademarks remain the property of their respective owners, bear no association with the author or the publisher, and are used for fictional purposes only.

Library of Congress Cataloging-in-Publication Data
Jones, Eddie.
The Day The World Sneezed / Eddie Jones 2nd ed.

Printed in the United States of America

DEDICATION

This book is dedicated to my cousin Ricky who practiced the art of "social distancing" long before it became a thing.

ELMER CLEARS OUT

Thursday, March 12, 2020, 4:53 p.m.

On the day the man from the Bureau of Land Management came to his farm, Elmer was out back banging on a plow. The clang of metal against metal reverberated throughout the barn, which meant the phone ringing in the house went unanswered.

Elmer saw no need to own a phone he could carry. His wife Edith, though, had other ideas about technology. Before she passed, she'd gossip on her phone for hours. This was fine with Elmer because, if Edith was talking on her phone, she wasn't bothering him. When Edith died, Elmer buried the little phone with her—placed it right next to her ear on the silk pillow the funeral home had tossed in with the purchase of her casket. He thought the phone added a nice touch.

When the house phone stopped ringing, Elmer turned his attention back to the plow.

The intruder came strolling around the side of the house and continued toward the wide doorway of the barn, prompting Elmer to wipe the grease from his hands. The bent plow would have to wait.

Elmer bumped up the bill of his cap. "Hep ya?"

"Ricks, with the Bureau of Land Management. Got a minute?"

With the sun setting in the west, casting a harsh glare in the stranger's eyes, Elmer got a good look at his visitor. Oily hair, backs of hands and cheeks tanned from the sun … a faint, brown stain of sweat along the inside of the collar of his white shirt.

Elmer felt certain the man was lying about his credentials. Elmer's third cousin, Malcolm, worked for the Bureau of Land Management out of the New Mexico office. If someone from BLM were coming to see Elmer, he felt certain Malcolm would have called to give him a heads up. Then again, the phone in the house had been ringing, and more than once.

"Rumor has it you're stockpiling Lysol," said the man. "Thought we should talk about that."

"Got some lye soap," said Elmer. "Can give yah a bar if you want."

"No, this would be Lysol spray I'm asking about. It's used to clean things?"

"Water and lye soap cleans pretty good," Elmer replied.

"So, no Lysol, then? No hoarding of cleaning supplies of any kind?"

Hoarding? The man's tone—and his interest in Lysol—struck Elmer as peculiar, as did the long drive out to his farm. Elmer's gaze shifted from the man toward the white Ford pickup parked next to his home. Lime-green stripe down its side with a BLM Fire logo on the driver's door … emergency light bar on the cab roof. A hefty-looking vehicle for someone asking about cleaning supplies. Malcolm drove one of them electric cars that moved so slowly it couldn't get out of its own way.

"If I was to come across some of this lye stuff," Elmer said, "what'd it be worth to you?"

"Lysol. And depends. A case of six gallons? Maybe, say, a hundred."

Elmer did the math. He wasn't exactly sure what Edith had paid per case for the Lysol he needed to clean his slaughterhouse, but he was pretty sure it wasn't anywhere close to a hundred dollars. If the Bureau man was offering a Benjamin Franklin for each case, that meant Elmer's stash was worth a heap more on the street.

"What you need it for?" Elmer asked.

"Official government business."

"Procurement," Elmer replied.

"Excuse me?"

"You'll need a requisition form." Elmer gave the man a long, hard stare. "I served in the 266th Quartermaster Battalion. Nothing moved in or out with a requisition form."

"I'm sure you know during a national emergency that hoarding vital medical supplies is a crime."

"News to me. Come across some," Elmer asked, "is there a way I can contact you?"

The Bureau man offered Elmer a business card. "Text me at that number."

Elmer studied the card. P. Ricks: Bureau of Land Management. There was a number, but no address. "Text you say?"

"To that number."

Staring at the phone number, Elmer wondered about the man's instructions. Not wanting to give the fellow a reason to hang around any longer, he tucked the card into his hip pocket.

"Interfering with official government business can have serious consequences," said the Bureau man. "Impoundment of vehicles, for example, or in some instances forfeiture of property."

Elmer gazed across the vast acres of his farm and thought back to riding in his daddy's lap on the tractor, the smell of Daddy's sweat in his coveralls and flannel shirts; the pair playing catch in the backyard and the crack of the bat as his father hit fly balls for him. He hated to think that some government bureaucrat would steal his place over some cleaning supplies his wife bought.

"If you come across some you might've, ah… forgotten about… text me right away," said the Bureau man. "It's a matter of national interest."

Elmer had his doubts about that last part. If there was one thing Elmer had learned in his eighty-two years, it was that if the government wanted something, it took it.

He stepped back inside the barn. "If I come across some of this lye soil stuff, I'll surely let you know."

"Make sure you do."

As the Bureau man's BLM truck disappeared down the highway, Elmer began to clear out. Staying wasn't an option. Taking a quick inventory of the boxes stacked to the ceiling, Elmer made a mental note of the date the man from the Bureau of Land Management visited his farm: Thursday, March 12, 2020.

A day and date that would change his life forever.

MAKING A CLEAN GETAWAY

Thursday, March 12, 2020, 5:23 p.m.

The Lysol spray was Edith's idea. Back when they still had hogs, she'd driven their truck into town for slaughterhouse supplies. Then one day she came home murmuring about OneStopShop, a place where you could "order on the web" and they'd deliver to your house—same way Harvey's Hardware had done before Mr. Harvey died.

"From now on we're getting our stuff from OneStopShop," Edith had announced.

Three days later, a large box arrived with a smiley face on its side. Elmer peeked inside and found a whole case of Lysol. The next day another box showed up filled with hand wipes. Elmer carried it to the barn and got to work on the meat locker.

Within weeks, OneStopShop became Elmer's favorite word. When the TP ran low, he'd leave an empty roll on the counter. Days later, boxes arrived.

After Edith died, Elmer thought about contacting OneStopShop to see if he could reduce the frequency of his orders, but couldn't find a phone number in any of the boxes. He wondered if he ought to wait on the porch for the delivery driver. Surely he could prevail upon the young fellow to stop or slow the shipments. But the boxes with the smiley face reminded Elmer of Edith, so he let things be.

Then he ran out of space in the barn. The loft was full of Lysol, as were the seed bins below. Elmer had no choice. The time had come to ditch OneStopShop. He wrote a note and left it on the porch.

My wife died. No need to keep coming. – Elmer.

A month passed, then another, without any further shipments. With his stock of TP running low, he drove to town and looked for the brand Edith used to get from OneStopShop. He settled for a generic single-ply brand with a rough texture.

That evening he sat in his rocker and stared toward the highway, missing Edith's smiley-face boxes.

Elmer returned to beating the bent plow. Cases and cases of cleaning supplies stood stacked to the rafters. Elmer needed a plan. The Bureau man would be back, and the thought of them taking Edith's stash left him riled.

The memory of Edith's voice, warm but chiding, mocked him. *Remember, before I got sick when I used to tell you we should sell this place and travel? But you wouldn't budge.*

Elmer bumped up the bill of his cap and stared at the loft overhead. "I know, I know. You were after me to explore the national parks, but I got a pretty good patch of land right here."

You should have trusted me, Elmer. The Lord helps us count our days so we can set our hearts on livin' wise. Now I'm gone, you're there, and those parks are still waiting.

"What are you saying, Edith?"

We talked about this, hon. Wouldn't it be nice to help those who don't have what we got? The least. The left out. The overlooked.

He squinted at the tower of supplies. "I suppose so."

Then why are you still bangin' on that plow? Get moving.

Elmer set down the hammer, went to the house, and phoned his sister. "You still driving long haul?"

"Hello to you too, brother."

"That R Model Mack rig of yours, it still runs good?"

"What do you need, Elmer? Spit it out."

"I got a delivery that needs moving. Can you be here first thing in the morning?"

"Bake a mess of cheese biscuits for me. I'll see you at sunrise."

"CORONAVIRUS"—GET USED TO HEARING ABOUT IT

Friday, March 13, 2020, 6:49 a.m.

Outside Hayes, Kansas, Elmer and Trudy pulled into a truck stop to refuel.

Elmer welcomed the stop. Trudy had talked for the past hour about people on television who were, in her words, "loud, rude, and needed their mouths washed out with soap."

"Politicians and reporters," she went on. "You can't trust them and can't shut them up."

Elmer found himself secretly grateful that the day after Edith's funeral, he had accidentally mowed over the line from the antenna to the house. With the TV switched off, the home's sudden silence at first left him missing Edith more than he could bear, but in time, he found himself talking out loud to her. Their chats seemed to help pass the time.

Inside the truck stop, Elmer scanned magazine and newspaper headlines. He missed keeping up with what was going on in the world, but not enough to pay for the discouraging articles published by news conglomerates. Given their destination and Trudy's nonstop yacking, he grabbed a stack of reading material.

At the counter he noticed most non-truckers wore face masks. Elmer owned sprayer masks he used for herbicide. It had never occurred to him to wear one in public.

Back in the rig, Elmer asked, "What's up with the masks?"

"Coronavirus," Trudy answered.

"Something you get from drinking beer?"

Trudy tapped a headline on the *Wichita Beagle*. "Read and learn, Brother."

Elmer organized the newspapers in his lap. The magazines he saved for later when they reached the Rockies and the winding roads.

Trudy worked her way through the gears, accelerating onto the interstate ramp. Elmer took in the view out the window. At his age, every trip, no matter how long or short, might be his last.

"You look deep in thought," Trudy said. "What's on your mind?"

Without looking up, he replied, "There's talk Major League Baseball may have to pause or cancel this season because of some sickness."

"Coronavirus. And no, you can't get it from drinking beer."

"Maybe it's just as well. The Royals only won fifty-eight games the year before last and fifty-nine last season."

Trudy merged into traffic on the interstate and asked, "Do you remember when Mom made that Royals uniform for you?"

"Best birthday present ever."

"You were pretty good at baseball. I forget why you gave it up."

He slumped. "Not good enough."

"But you made the league all-star team almost every year."

"That was farm kids. The game got a lot tougher when I hit high school and started playing against the best in the county."

"I think you'd have been just fine," Trudy said. "You were quick. They almost never threw you out when you stole a base."

Speeding past rows of winter wheat, Elmer said, "I never told anyone this, but when I was twelve, I mentioned to Dad how one day I'd play for the Royals. He looked at me with this sad expression and said, 'Elmer, a guy your size is going to have a tough go of it. You're a good hitter, but in the majors, everyone can hit and homer. You should focus on enjoying this right now because one day you'll look back on all the fun and miss it.

"Dad said that?"

He picked at a scab on the back of his hand. "Dad didn't mean anything by it. Was just telling it like it was."

"But you outworked everyone."

"Hustle and heart aren't enough. The big, strong, and fast… those with God-given natural ability get a shot. Little guys like me get shot down. Speaking of getting shot down, how long before this rig of yours shuts down for good? It's what, nearly forty years old?"

"Forty-two, but I keep it maintained."

"It ought to be in a museum."

"It's paid for and parts are still available," Trudy said. "Can't afford anything nicer."

"Still stingy, like always."

"Frugal, Brother, like you."

The Kansas horizon bled red in the grip of a rising sun, promising a glorious day on the highway.

"Okay, fess up," said Trudy. "What's in the boxes?"

Unfolding a newspaper, he answered, "This and that."

"Must be mighty important, you asking for my help."

The rhythmic rumble of the tires jostled the paper in his lap. "You still living with your friend?"

"Carol. And yes."

Elmer rubbed his chin, his gaze shifting to Trudy's left hand on the wheel. "Um."

"Don't start or I'll put you out right here."

Elmer turned a page. "Says here officials are so worried about the disease spreading that the World Health Organization's in panic mode."

"'Panic mode?' They said that?"

"Guess journalism isn't what it used to be."

"You ever thought of selling the farm and moving someplace with people nearby?"

He glanced at the rearview mirror and the road behind them.

"You can't keep the farm forever," Trudy said. "There's going to come a time when you'll need care, and care costs money. It's the perfect spot for a subdivision. Close to town, but not in town."

"I'm not selling the farm," Elmer said.

"Why not? The place is paid off, and the property taxes are low."

Elmer eyed the dashboard. "This cab got a radio?"

"Hardheaded to the end," Trudy said, then pushed buttons on the dashboard.

"Dad said, 'If it ain't broke, don't break it.'"

"And look where it got him? An early grave," said Trudy. "If just once he'd taken Mom's advice and gone to a doctor, he might have lived another twenty years."

"And been miserable the whole time. We can't know the future, Sis. Best to live each day as if it's our last."

"This from the boy who quit baseball because he was afraid of getting cut from his high school team."

"Turn it up. I want to hear what this feller says about the sickness."

"Coronavirus, Brother. Best get used to saying it."

ANOTHER TURBULENT DAY WITH THE CORONAVIRUS

Friday, March 13, 2020, 7:01 a.m.

From the truck's radio, a male with a deep voice said, "Welcome to National Public News. I'm Steve Green. After another turbulent day on Wall Street, we begin today with news out of Washington, where concerns about the coronavirus pandemic continue to ripple across the globe. Just days after meeting with the daughter of the American president and other US officials, yesterday an Australian government minister tested positive for the virus."

With a glance in Trudy's direction, Elmer asked, "Is that rich feller still president?"

"You know better than to ask. I'm not talking politics with you." Trudy turned the volume up on the radio. "Sends my blood pressure through the roof."

"Elsewhere in the United States," the announcer continued, "public life appears to be grinding to a halt. In New York, Broadway theaters went dark, and major theme parks, like Disneyland and Disney World, say they are closing. Six governors ordered schools shuttered statewide. Professional soccer and hockey leagues suspended their seasons, this one day after the NBA's announcement that it was indefinitely suspending all league play. Major League Baseball has postponed Opening Day until further notice. But perhaps the biggest news in sports is that the NCAA announced its March Madness basketball tournament is canceled."

Elmer asked, "You still follow K.U. basketball?"

"Do the Jayhawks rock chalk? They're top-ranked but facing some recruiting violation and might be banned from the Tournament."

"Edith sure enjoyed watching her Jayhawks."

"That why you put in that big satellite dish I saw in the yard?"

"After she got sick, Edith couldn't leave the house much. I had my VHS tapes from when I subscribed to that outfit that shipped shows each week, but Edith wanted more than *Hee Haw*."

"You're a dinosaur, Brother."

The NPN reporter continued. "Other countries have imposed new travel restrictions and bans on public gatherings. In Nepal, climbing expeditions on Mount Everest have been canceled. And on Wall Street, yesterday's stunning meltdown erased all the stock market gains made since the president's surprise election four years ago. To date, there have been nearly 140,000 cases of coronavirus and over 5,000 deaths. Health officials warn we are still in the early stages of this deadly pandemic."

"Seriously, Elmer, what's in the boxes? I need to know if we get stopped."

"Tell'em it's farm supplies."

"It didn't smell like farm supplies when I helped you load my trailer. What it smelled like was Lysol."

Elmer removed his cap and rubbed away a sheen of sweat from his forehead. "How long a drive to Browning?"

Trudy scanned the dashboard gauges, checked mirrors, and said, "Day or so. I have to build in time to stop and sleep."

There was always the slim chance Trudy would drive straight through. The sooner they got Elmer's truckload of Lysol to its destination, the sooner the knot in his gut would unwind.

"Law still require mandatory rest breaks?" he asked.

"You ever know a time when the government stopped requiring something?"

"Wouldn't want you to break the law on my account," he said. "Best do like you're supposed to."

As a short NPN promo spot concluded, reporter Green came back on the air. "The Centers for Disease Control and Prevention warns it's getting harder to find cleaning supplies, especially for hospitals and assisted living facilities,"

"Edith was a saint for putting up with you," said Trudy. "My trucker friends are saying OneStopShop can't keep up with demand, and here you are with a full load of much-needed cleaning supplies. You ought to feel guilty."

"What I feel is anxious to get to Browning. The sooner I don't have anything anyone wants, the faster I can get back to being left alone."

"You really quit on baseball? That's so not like the big brother I remember."

"Not every dream is meant to be."

"If you're looking for a dream to scrap, I'd pick this trip to Browning. I got a good idea of what you have in mind, and from where I sit behind this wheel, the odds of you pulling this off are long to none."

"You stick to driving. I'll worry 'bout what comes when we get there."

"You mean if we get there. Given that right after we pulled out of your drive, we came upon that BLM truck not more than a mile from your house, I'm betting your bureau man knows you're on the run. And if so, that would explain those blue lights in my rear-view mirror." Trudy jabbed a thumb over her shoulder. "Farm supplies? That's what you want me to say if I'm pulled?"

"It's not a lie," Elmer answered.

"Maybe not, but if you know what they're after, is it really the truth?"

COLLEGE BASKETBALL CANCELLED

Saturday, March 14, 2020, 7:14 a.m.

Sometime after midnight, they stopped at a truck stop in Buffalo, Wyoming, so Trudy could sleep. A multi-vehicle wreck with fatalities outside of Denver had set them back a good amount of time. Now with the sky turning pink in the east and Trudy snoring in the sleeping compartment, Elmer roused himself from the passenger seat and crawled from the cab.

With it still dark out and colder than he would have liked, Elmer hiked into town and took a table at the Busy Bee. "Fresh cantaloupe and a cheese biscuit. And orange juice if you have it."

"All out," his waitress replied. "Don't expect to get more anytime soon."

"Then just coffee."

"Also out."

Elmer wondered how a place that served breakfast could be out of coffee and orange juice and expect to stay in business.

"Water?"

"Coming right up," she answered.

It dawned on Elmer that his waitress wore a white face mask. In fact, other than Elmer, every person in the Busy Bee wore a mask. Made him sort of wish he'd thought to bring one of his sprayer masks just so he wouldn't stand out.

When the waitress returned with his water, Elmer asked, "Sick?"

"Not yet, and don't plan to be."

The way she answered made Elmer wonder if the virus was a bigger deal than he'd thought—maybe even as big as when those two planes hit the buildings in New York. He asked for directions to the nearest bank, finished eating, and left a ten-dollar bill under his empty water glass.

A pile of individually wrapped masks lay on a table inside the lobby of the Great Northern Bank. A professionally printed sign demanded all visitors wear a mask, wipe their hands with hand wipes, and then visit the restroom to wash their hands with soap and water for twenty-four seconds. From the looks of things, the world appeared to be losing its mind.

Elmer did as instructed. He was, if anything, a rule-follower—up to a point.

Back in the lobby, a loan officer led him to her office. The visit by the Bureau man had set Elmer's mind to wondering what else the government might try to take from him. While packing for the trip, he had placed some personal papers and extra sets of keys in the bank-teller pouch Edith once used for receipts.

"I need you to watch me officially sign these papers," he said.

"You mean notarized?"

"Yes, ma'am, that one."

Examining the papers, she said, "Guess you heard we're now in a bear market."

Elmer had not heard, but talking through the mask made his upper lip sweat, so he let her comment pass.

"Just like that," she continued, "a twenty percent drop from its high just a week ago. A historical drop like that and at that speed—never happened before."

"Strange times," was all Elmer could come up with.

"People's life savings were wiped out in the blink of an eye. What a mess."

Elmer, trying to appear friendly, said, "The only market I know about is the grain market. It's been getting worse ever since big industry took over. Time was a feller put in a hard day's work, he'd have something to show for it." Licking the sweat from the top of his lip, he continued. "Now you got all them corporations buying up land and using hybrid seed. Stuff grows well enough and all, but I ain't exactly convinced it's good to eat."

The bank lady looked up from the papers and made eye contact. "The previous fastest stock market drop? Twenty-eight days, 1929. We're in uncharted territory here."

Elmer hoped he would reach the end of this uncharted territory in another day or so. But to do so required the bank lady to mosey along a little faster. By now, Trudy would be up, washed, and eager to roll.

The bank lady held the stamp over the first paper in the pile, then hesitated. "Is the beneficiary aware of these terms?"

"Probably not. Do they need to be?"

She tapped signature lines on each sheet. "Sign here, here, here …" and then pushed the papers back across the desk. "The good news is, a year after the market's other historic drops, 1998, '87, and '90, the market went back up twenty-three, twenty-eight, and thirty-eight percent."

Elmer scrawled his full name on each line, then handed them back for her to review.

"The market took a little longer to bounce back after the Great Depression," she continued, "though I doubt I'm telling you something you don't already know. I suspect your parents lived through it."

Elmer's parents had, in fact, survived the Great Depression. It was one reason he ate leftovers until he spied or tasted mold and kept tools and household items that no longer worked. Never know when you might need a backup, and with a little tinkering, he could repair most things.

She stamped each sheet, then handed the papers back to Elmer.

He peeled off a hundred-dollar bill and handed it to her. "This cover it?"

Standing, she said, "Be right back with your change."

"No need. Put what's left over in that bucket out there for them sick kids."

On his walk from the bank back to the truck stop, Elmer passed a small, two-story motel no bigger than his home. A sign in the window advertised that Butch Cassidy and the Sundance Kid had once slept there. Though tempted to step inside and explore the Old West artifacts in the front parlor, he kept walking. A long day in uncharted territory lay ahead.

"Ever stayed at the Occidental Hotel?"

At the question, Elmer turned to find a young man straddling a bike.

Without prompting, the young man continued, "Dude, the Hoover Suite is so cool. That's my fav room. There's this radical picture on the wall showing the Hole in the Wall Gang chillin' in the front parlor. You gotta snap a selfie with it, man. The staff's cool with it. Tourists do it all the time!"

Elmer ruminated on that a bit. "I know the movie," Elmer said, hoping that would end the chat. "Saw it with my wife. It was okay."

"Seriously? Just okay? That movie's a classic, bro!"

"I should be getting along," Elmer replied.

"And Longmire. You gotta check it out, too."

Fearing he would regret asking, Elmer replied, "What about Longmire?"

"So check this out. It's like this rad crime drama based on these gnarly mystery novels by Craig Johnson and it's set right here in Buffalo. They call the town something else on the show, but we're famous. His daughter Cady pushes him to be the new deputy of this out-of-the-way town, and he does, and he likes it so much he decides to run for re-election and wins, and then with a little help from his main dude, Henry Standing Bear, he starts piecing his life back together."

"Um, hum."

"It's like this epic journey of redemption. If you've never watched it, you have to binge, bro."

It had been years since Elmer binged on anything other than *Hee Haw*, and at his age, he wasn't about to go back to those days. Pretending to catch the vibe, Elmer replied, "I'll do that, bro," and attempted to walk away.

Straddling his bike, the young man joined Elmer, riding slowly beside him. "Guess you heard about Gonzaga. They were straight-up killing it this season. Cruising through the WCC like it's no biggie, racking up a killer record of thirty-one and two. That's some epic, next-level dominance, you know what I'm saying? Then college basketball gets cancelled because of the coronavirus. When it comes to respect, the Zags don't always get the love they deserve."

"I'm heading to the truck stop," Elmer said. "You?"

"I got nowhere to be. Slow Saturday in Buffalo. Most days are."

At the end of the block, Elmer turned the corner and spied the truck stop sign above the rooftops.

"I mean, imagine the hype if Mark Few and the crew had snagged this year, bro. It would've been legendary! Total bummer."

Though vaguely familiar with Gonzaga, Elmer felt certain they would be no match for Edith's Jayhawks. "Right, bro. Total bummer."

A state patrol cruiser blew past the pair, its blue lights flashing, siren wailing.

"The coronavirus is wrecking everything," said the young man. "I mean, they had to cancel the tourney, sure, but still. … A billion bucks in revenue, gone just like that! This could seriously change college sports forever, dude."

Another state patrol cruiser raced toward them. The lump in Elmer's gut tightened into a double knot.

His gaze fixed on the patrol car racing past, the young man said, "Something's definitely going down. There's, like, never this much action in Buffalo."

Coming to a major intersection, Elmer turned toward the road that led to the truck stop. "Sorry 'bout your team."

Elmer sincerely meant it. Other than Kansas, in basketball, Elmer always pulled for the little guy.

"Hopefully, they'll crush it next year. Gotta stay positive, right?" Offering Elmer an outstretched fist, he added, "Appreciate the good vibe, bro."

Elmer hesitated, then bumped knuckles with the young man, and walked toward the vast parking lot of trucks. Keeping his head down, focused on his feet, he reached Trudy's rig. A patrol car was parked near the entrance closest to the fuel islands. Another near the second entrance. The double-knotted lump in Elmer's gut left him feeling queasy.

The law's onto me, he thought. The Bureau man must have tipped them off about Edith's stash of Lysol.

Taking a seat on the steps beneath the passenger door of the rig, he pulled out a free copy of the *Buffalo Bulletin*, courtesy of the Busy Bee.

The paper's lead article reported that a US government official had complained that China was withholding shipments of "much-needed medicines to treat the coronavirus." According to the article, all American pharmaceutical companies had shut down their U.S. manufacturing facilities years ago and moved production to China, leaving the U.S. vulnerable to pandemics and unable to ramp up production on short notice.

To Elmer's way of thinking, it seemed foolish for the U.S. government to blame China. If you teach your neighbor how to plow, sow, and harvest, you have to know that one day he'll undercut you on price and put you out of business. But Edith was always saying helping others is the neighborly thing to do.

The news article concluded by saying that Chinese officials were demanding that America, and the president in particular, issue an apology to China. The article reported that the president had offered a two-word response, which could not be printed in the paper.

Ballsy, Elmer thought. That'll get him some votes.

"Hey, mister, can you help me?"

Elmer looked toward the rear of the rig. Peeping from behind the back of the truck, a man about forty years of age, in a blue blazer, slacks, and loafers, waved to him.

"What sort of help you need?" Elmer asked.

"It's for my father. They're holding him hostage because of the coronavirus and I need you to help me bust him out."

LOCKDOWN AND LOCKED OUT— NO VISITORS FOR PATIENTS DUE TO COVID-19

Saturday, March 14, 2020, 10:27 a.m.

"Hostage?" Confused, Elmer looked at the young man. "You mean like terrorists or gangs?"

"No. The nursing home," he answered. "We need to get him out and someplace safe. No one would suspect he's riding in a tractor trailer."

Elmer shook his head. "Wish I could, but we're on a tight schedule."

"Please, mister. People in that home are sick and dying, and they're not letting anyone leave. If you don't help, my dad is done for."

What are you doing still standing there?

Elmer silently answered his wife. *Not getting involved.*

You know what I'd do?

I'm not you, Edith. And my sister's already doing me a big favor by loaning me her truck.

If you want others to do unto you…

Elmer sighed the way a leaky air cushion might under the weight of Charles Barkley. "How far's this place?" Elmer asked.

"Couple of blocks." Pivoting, the young man jogged across the road. Elmer hurried to catch up.

Two blocks from the truck stop, at the Buffalo Assisted Living, a plump woman, who appeared to be in her fifties, stood among bushes next to the building. Banging on a window, she kept yelling, "Mamma, it's me, Lila May!"

With her face pressed to the glass, a frail woman appeared in the window. Dressed in a nightgown, she placed her palms against the glass as though pleading to be let out. Only then, as if in a scene from a zombie film, did Elmer notice other people standing at windows.

"Our father checked in three weeks ago for physical therapy. But then the coronavirus hit and they cancelled all visitations. It's like a prison: no one is getting in or out. I'm Scott, by the way."

"Elmer." He bumped up the bill of his cap and glanced back towards the truck stop. "Not sure I can do much for you. Don't have much experience with breaking and entering."

"Dad fell off his bike," Scott continued, "and he's rehabbing a broken ankle and a banged-up knee. We chat on the phone each day. He hasn't gotten out of bed in two weeks. They don't have the staff to tend to him and he's losing his mobility. Lying in that bed all day and doing nothing is killing him. I have a plan to get him out, but it'll take both of us."

"A plan?"

"I visited him almost every day before they locked down the place. Not once did I see anyone wearing a mask."

Ah, there was that dreaded word again. "What did you have in mind?"

"You're maybe old enough to remember," said Scott. "Ever watch *The Great Escape*?"

"Oh, sure. A bunch of fellas are stuck in a Nazi POW camp and start digging tunnels. They get all sneaky, making fake IDs, tailoring their uniforms to look like the Germans, and setting up a forgery operation. Then, one night, they start crawling out like groundhogs. Steve McQueen jumps a fence on a motorcycle. As I recall, not many make it out."

"Okay, maybe not the best example," Scott said, "but the plan is to do something like that."

Though the escape did not involve a motorcycle, it did include a motorized scooter, a swiped ID from one of the staff, a pizza delivered by Elmer, and several staff members backing away as he pressed his way into the facility—without a mask. The distraction gave Scott time to scale the eight-foot high wooden fence that separated the courtyard area from the sidewalk.

By the time Scott, his father, and Elmer reached Trudy's truck, she had the engine idling and a scowl that suggested sleep had not improved her demeanor.

"Not riding in my cab, they're not."

"We're only driving them across town," Elmer explained.

Scott joined them. "Going to stash some of Dad's things in my car," he said. "Be right back."

"If the old guy's son has a car, why do they need to ride with us?"

"Too much heat," Elmer replied. "The staff knows Scott's vehicle."

"Fine. They can ride in the back with your Lysol."

The old man arrived on his motorized scooter. "Name's Jim. Thanks for doing this. Been in Buffalo long?"

"Passing through," Elmer answered. "Dad brought me here as a kid. He took me to Fort Kearny and told me about how soldiers fought to keep the Bozeman Trail open for folks heading to Montana in search of gold." Elmer's tone softened. "Place like this holds memories for me, you know. I made a good living farming, but long before the deed was mine, it belonged to Native Americans. A person can go a long time before realizing they got debts to repay."

"Elmer, the man was only being polite," said Trudy, "not asking for your life's story."

"Thanks for getting me out of there," Jim said. "A few more days and I might not have made it."

"That bad?" Elmer asked.

"Residents and staff are dropping faster than the stock market."

"This is a bad idea," said Trudy. "Bonehead stupid bad. If those boxes shift and fall, the two of them are gonna get smashed."

With the pair safely inside, Elmer pulled the door down and latched it. "So drive slow."

Seated in the cab, her hand on the shifter, Trudy said, “This is kidnapping.”

“More like rescuing in my book.”

“Only thing I know for certain is it’s illegal and we’re a long way from Kansas, Brother.”

BONEHEAD STUPID DUMB

Saturday, March 14, 2020, 10:53 a.m.

"I think I heard them yelling," Elmer said. "Did you hear yelling? We need to stop."

Sighing more loudly than normal, Trudy asked, "Stop where?"

During their brief time traveling together, Elmer had noticed that the long, deep exhalations of the truck's air brakes were only slightly noisier than Trudy's displeasure with whatever Elmer did or suggested.

"We're a big rig pulling a trailer, Brother. We can't simply stop by the curb."

"That shoulder up there by the exit ramp, pull off long enough for me to see if Scott and Jim are okay."

Trudy slowed the truck and eased onto the dirt shoulder. If things worked out as he hoped, Elmer might move to Buffalo, Wyoming. Living in a town where Butch and Sundance once hung outmatched his new Old West vibe—though he hoped his ending worked out better than the two outlaws.

Elmer raised the trailer's rear door enough to see that legs and arms and a hand were poking out from between two boxes.

Trudy came around from the driver's side to lend a hand. "Dumb idea. Bonehead stupid."

"You took that turn too fast. I told you to go slow." Offering a hand, he said to their stowaways, "Either of you hurt?"

Scott crawled from beneath the boxes. "Don't think so. Just bruised a little."

"Let's get you two out and upfront."

"No way," said Trudy. "Told you they're not riding in the cab. Without seatbelts, we have a wreck. They could get killed."

"So, don't wreck. Like I keep saying, we need to take it slow."

"And you need to stop using 'we' in this bonehead stupid escape of yours. I never agreed to this."

Together, Elmer and Scott got Jim down from the truck. "Sorry 'bout this," Elmer said to Jim. "I begged my sister to take it easy."

"No need to apologize. I'm just thankful to be out of that death trap."

By the time Trudy re-stacked the load and filled the gap where the pair had sat, father and son were squeezed into the cab's sleeping compartment with the curtain closed. Pulling off the shoulder and onto the ramp, Trudy raced through the gears in a way that let Elmer know she was none too happy with him.

Hoping to smooth things over, he said, "High school tryouts were the worst for me."

Trudy shot him a look. "Worst in what way?"

"Freshman year, I saw all these boys I'd played against, some on the all-star teams, others from parts of the county I'd never even heard of. Dad was right. I was the smallest of the group and there were forty of us trying to make a fifteen-man squad."

Jim peeked out from behind the curtain. "You played ball?"

"Catcher and right field," Elmer answered.

"So what did you do?" Trudy asked.

"I couldn't face being cut again. I'd already tried out for basketball and football and hadn't made it. By then I'd learned the drill. High school coaches have their favorites. Once an athlete, always an athlete." Elmer addressed Jim. "I pretended to dress out for practice, but I sneaked off to a grocery store down the road. I hung out there until practice ended, then walked back, rubbed dirt on my pants and jersey, and waited for Mom to pick me up. When the cuts came, I told Dad I didn't make it. Dad already thought I wouldn't make it, so he wasn't surprised."

"I've got blue lights behind me," said Trudy. "If I lose my license over this harebrained scheme of yours, you'll wish you'd never heard of Lysol."

"I wondered if that's what I was smelling," Scott said. "Man, Lysol is like gold. Some of the staff at that Coronavirus concentration camp where Dad was staying complained that they couldn't get enough."

Trudy hit her blinker and downshifted, aiming for the upcoming exit ramp.

"Says here in the Buffalo Bulletin," Elmer read aloud, "that the Secretary of HHS has issued a notice designating health and medical supplies as protected from price gouging."

A state trooper patrol car shot past, continuing up the interstate. "Thank God," Trudy said under her breath.

"Amen," Jim replied.

"Article goes on to say that masks, shields, gloves, respirators, ventilators, medical gowns, disinfecting devices, and clinical-grade disinfectant products are in short supply. And I'm quoting: 'March 18, the President invoked the Defense Production Act, making it illegal to stockpile items such as sanitizing products that exceed reasonable demands for business, personal, or home consumption.' Goes on to say that this also prohibits the resale of products at prices that exceed prevailing market prices." Looking up from the newspaper, Elmer said, "You think that trooper was looking for us?"

Trudy replied, "Elmer, check my phone and see if there's a wreck up ahead."

"Uh, oh," Jim groaned. "I'm getting an Amber alert on my phone."

"Take the next exit," Scott said, "then right at the top of the ramp."

"It's me." Jim showed his phone to Scott. "The facility has reported me missing."

"This exit?" Trudy asked.

"No! Keep driving!" Scott said. "I'll text my sister to meet us."

"Me? Do what with your phone?" Elmer asked.

"My sister lives twenty miles north in Sheridan. Dad can stay at her place 'till we sort things out."

"Smooth move, Ex-Lax, busting a patient out of a rehab facility, Brother. Bonehead stupid."

"Never know when you might be the answer to someone's cry for help."

"From now on, keep your sentimental intentions on a bumper sticker and out of my truck."

FAR AWAY FROM THERE

Saturday, March 14, 2020, 1:45 p.m.

In Sheridan, Wyoming, Trudy pulled her rig into a big-box store parking lot to wait for Jim's daughter.

"You stay with these two," said Trudy. "I'm going to get a few things."

"What sort?"

"The sort that's none of your business."

Which, of course, to Elmer meant Trudy needed to shop for women's stuff. Edith used to say things like that when Elmer nosed a little too far into her business.

"Only asking," Elmer replied, "because there's maybe some stuff I need."

"Try to keep from getting arrested," said Trudy, stepping from the cab. "And don't let our hostage run off."

Since leaving Buffalo, Jim had not made a sound other than a steady and healthy-sounding snore.

Scott crawled from the sleeping compartment and dropped into the driver's seat. "I'm going to step out and see if I can spot my sister's car."

"She call?"

"No." Scott opened the driver's door and stepped down. "But she texted to say she was pulling into the parking lot."

Out the front windshield, vehicles whizzed past the big-box-store parking lot. Since leaving Buffalo, Elmer hadn't seen any sheriff's cars or state troopers—a good sign, he hoped. As was the case in the truck stop and in Buffalo, people in the parking lot wore face masks. Taking advantage of the solitude, he returned to reading his newspaper. Midway through an article on how much revenue Major League Baseball was set to lose due to Coronavirus, the driver's door swung open.

"Stupid store." Trudy crawled into the cab empty-handed, her face one of someone who had missed out on a big sale. "Place looks as if they're going out of business. Shelves are empty. You name it, they're sold out. Canned goods, frozen foods, fresh vegetables … toilet paper. It's like the start of Armageddon."

"What did you need? Maybe I packed it." Elmer was thinking of a razor. He had noticed a few whiskers on his sister's upper lip. Not that he intended to share his Mach 3 with Trudy, but sometimes he kept a cheap disposable in the side pocket of his duffle bag.

"Never you mind," Trudy replied. "You see that sister yet?"

"Scott's out there looking for her now."

"We should have never agreed to take along these two."

Continuing to scan headlines and articles, Elmer commented without looking up, "Says here that by mid-April, the CDC is expecting more than 7,000 deaths in nursing homes. Busting Jim out was the right thing to do, Sis."

"I've complained for years that our government doesn't do enough to take care of the elderly."

"Well, sure, it does seem like there's a plan in place to slowly eliminate all the old people to make room for the young, but I don't think it's a conspiracy. More like bad bureaucratic bungling. This article says over 36,500 residents and employees tested positive for that virus. There is speculation that the death toll is a lot higher: that a good number of facilities aren't reporting cases or deaths."

"Here comes the son," said Trudy. "It's high time."

Elmer continued, "By mid-June, they're saying the number of deaths in nursing homes will soar past 50,000 dead and represent nearly half of the national death toll." Glancing across the parking lot, then at his sister, Elmer asked, "Where? I don't see him."

"Thought that was him. Guess not. Which way did he walk?"

"I didn't notice."

"Maybe he just walked off and ditched us?"

"With his dad in the cab? He wouldn't do that."

"And when I woke up this morning, I didn't think I'd become an accomplice to kidnapping."

Elmer peeked around the curtain. "He looks so peaceful. Jim sure seems to like sleeping in your cab."

"Don't start."

"Start what?"

"You know. And we're not taking him with us to Browning."

"Fine. If Scott doesn't return, we'll drop him off at a hospital."

"The old man's not a puppy, Elmer."

Trying to sound hopeful, he said, "According to the map and my calculations, Great Falls is only about four hours up the road. We're almost there."

"Elmer, we are nowhere near almost there. We're about as far from there as we can get." Trudy knuckled her eyes.

"I bet they got a good-size hospital in Great Falls that can take care of him. You and I can get a motel room for the night."

"Uh, oh. That doesn't look good," Elmer said.

Two sheriff cars came racing across the parking lot and screeched to a halt in front of the store. Jumping out, one ran up to a man in slacks and a white shirt.

"Don't tell me that's the son."

"That's not Scott," said Elmer. "He had on a blue blazer, remember?"

Trudy looked, then reached, into the sleeping compartment. "You mean this blue blazer?"

Cracking open his door, Elmer scanned behind the truck, then across the parking lot. No sign of Scott.

"Whoever it is, he's getting cuffed," said Trudy.

"Probably a shoplifter. You can never tell the good guys from the bad."

"Got that right. I'd never have suspected my brother to be a kidnapper."

"Hey, look! They took the cuffs off," Elmer said. "Told you, it's not Scott."

"No? Then how come he's pointing at us?"

While one officer remained with the man Elmer now suspected might, in fact, be Scott, the other hopped in his patrol car.

Trudy revved the engine, shifted into gear, and the truck began to roll. "You and your bonehead ideas."

"We saved a life. That's got to count for something."

Shifting into second gear, Trudy replied, "Oh, it's going to count, all right. I'll get fifteen to twenty for kidnapping." Blowing through a stop sign at the edge of the parking lot, Trudy said, "Look for someplace to hide."

"Hide an eighteen-wheel trailer?"

"Just look, okay?"

"Take a right, then the next right," Elmer said. "We'll park behind the store. They won't think to look for us."

"Bet they will, Brother. I'm sure of it."

DO DROP INN, BUT DON'T STAY

Saturday, March 14, 2020, 6:12 p.m.

Great Falls Do Drop Inn catered to truckers, and not affluent ones. Rigs and loads appeared to be more aligned with independent contractors and low-bid trucking fleets. The parking lot rumbled with seasoned vehicles past their prime, their paint jobs fading, and fenders chipped as if they'd seen one too many sunsets on the open road. Rust spots adorned exteriors like battle scars, proudly declaring their endurance through countless miles.

Elmer's gamble to elude the law had paid off. Parked behind the big-box store, they listened as sirens raced past and faded away.

But all Elmer's attempts to pick a nicer, fancier motel had failed to satisfy, so Trudy opted for a recommendation from her CB buddies. While she went inside to pay for two rooms with Elmer's credit card, he helped Jim from the cab and walked—but mostly carried—him inside.

On the lobby TV, a news reporter shielded his face while wind and snow blasted him. "If the country stops working and takes the next thirty days off, the economy is headed for a recession. Economists say the U.S. has never faced a moment quite like this. The impact of an economic shutdown may last years, or decades. Meanwhile, millions of Americans are bracing for weeks ahead with no school for their children and no clue how to juggle their jobs and childcare. There is a growing sense of dread about how to stay safe and sane amid the relentless spread of the coronavirus."

Trudy gave Elmer his room key. "We roll at 7:00 a.m."

Elmer gingerly settled Jim on a luggage cart and rolled him down the hall to their room, moved him from the cart to the bed, and then said, "Be right back. Need to return this."

On the lobby TV, a man in a heavy winter coat stood in front of a factory. "How am I supposed to pay my bills when my work hours just got cut by half? And how's my family supposed to plan for the future when I don't know if I'll have a job next week? This is crazy! I have friends desperate, like me, but with schools closed, we've all jumped on social media to find childcare. I'm not saying this is the end of the world. I'm not one of those whacko religious conspiracy nut jobs. But this sure looks like the end of the world."

Elmer offered a casual, "Times, they are a changin," to no one in particular, and hurried back to get Jim ready for bed.

In the room's minuscule bathroom, Elmer ran a tub of warm water and helped his guest out of his pants and underpants, shirt, and tee shirt. Cradling him like he had held Edith when she was near the end, he slowly lowered Jim into the tub.

Jim moaned.

"Too hot?" Elmer asked.

"I'll get used to it."

With a washrag and a fresh bar of soap, Elmer sponged Jim's chest and arms.

"Hate you have to wash me this way," Jim said. "I can almost reach everywhere, but not quite."

"Don't mind at all. Did the same for my wife for a while."

Long ago, Elmer had overcome his shyness of bathing someone who couldn't tend to themselves. Edith had not minded in the least that her husband cared for her with such tenderness, but at first, it had bothered Elmer. Before her sickness, he'd only seen his bride naked in moments of intimacy. Elmer's sudsy cleansing of her body became an act of love and one of the few ways he could still hold his bride without causing her pain—even if it did leave Elmer with a sad realization that the woman he'd promised to love until death was nearing the end.

Elmer dropped Jim's slightly soiled pants and underpants in the wastebasket by the toilet, then tied its plastic bag tight. Though Jim was a size smaller and certain to be swallowed by the outfit, Elmer felt sure his guest would get along fine in Elmer's extra pair of dungarees and Nebraska Huskers' sweatshirt.

"Hate my phone died," Jim said. "Didn't think to grab my charger when I left."

"My sister is trying to find a cord that can charge it. Soon as she does, she'll call Scott and tell him where you are."

He had no plans to lie. If pressed for details, Elmer would tell Jim the truth: his boy was most likely in custody. But so far, Scott's encounter with the law hadn't come up.

The constant stream of bleak news from the small TV left Elmer concerned. He feared that like an F5 tornado sweeping across the countryside, they might be in the path of a dark storm about to flatten them.

"Across the country, grocery stores have implemented measures to address the impact of COVID-19. Many have reduced their operating hours to discourage panic buying and allow staff sufficient time to restock shelves. Additionally, numerous fast-food chains, including Tippy Taco Time, have closed their dining rooms to prioritize the safety of customers and employees. Various states, including Georgia and Louisiana, have postponed their primary elections scheduled for April to mitigate the spread of the virus and ensure voter safety. The reluctance of some individuals to undergo COVID-19 testing has become a notable concern for government and health officials. Despite urgent pleas that those who may be sick get tested, there have been some instances where public figures, including President Trump, have refused."

Jim called from the bathroom, "I'm ready to get out."

"In the latest testament to the coronavirus pandemic's profound impact on daily life around the globe, Spain announced a nationwide lockdown."

"Be right there," Elmer replied.

"Meanwhile, France has closed all nonessential businesses, including cafes, restaurants, and movie theaters."

Elmer turned up the volume a smidge and, mindful of Jim's weakened state, carefully lifted him out of the bathtub. With a soft towel, he pressed the cloth to wrinkled skin, taking care to avoid the open wounds left by bed sores.

"Don't forget to pick up some antibiotics," Elmer said to himself. "Antibiotics, antibiotics, antibiotics."

He helped Jim into bed and said, "Got some chicken soup in a thermos. Packed it for the trip. Probably cold, but it's homemade and better than what you get in a convenience store." Elmer poured a small amount into the thermos cup and went back to watching the news.

On the screen, a brawl had broken out in the parking lot of a CostGo. Store employees were trying to break it up, but the scene reminded Elmer of the riots he'd witnessed after the incident at Kent State.

Sipping soup, Jim fixed his gaze on the screen and said, "A lot of people have it worse than me. My son says hospitals are overwhelmed and the staff are placing people in makeshift beds outside emergency rooms."

"I read an article in the *Buffalo Bulletin* that said Italy had experienced its biggest daily surge of patients ever." Elmer dabbed soup from the man's chin. "Claimed the wife of the Spanish prime minister, had tested positive for the sickness."

"Feels good to talk to someone. Thanks for getting me out of there."

"My wife would've done the same, only cared for you better."

On the television, a young girl from New York was talking to the camera, boasting about what it was like to feel invincible. "The bars in my neighborhood are all packed with people my age. Old people may be getting sick from this virus, but we're downing Coronas and partying like there's no tomorrow."

The camera cut to another reporter standing out front of Spokes Bicycle Shop in Leesburg, Virginia. The manager, Tim

Spokes, was saying, "A woman came in this morning and said, 'I normally go to the gym, but that's not happening right now, so I'm going to ride a bike and get my exercise outdoors.'"

"I rode a bicycle before I broke my ankle."

"So I heard," Elmer replied.

"God, I hope one day I get back to feeling like I did before I took that spill." Jim shifted onto his side and groaned. "I've never felt this bad, not ever. And I don't think this achiness is from my fall."

Elmer pressed the power button, turning off the set. "Things will get back to normal—someday."

When Elmer came out of the bathroom half an hour later, Jim lay snoring lightly.

Elmer killed the lights and started to pull the drapes closed, then stopped. A Great Falls police car sat parked next to Trudy's rig. With its lights flashing and a small crowd gathering nearby, an officer was walking to the back of the trailer.

Elmer's first thought was Jim's son. Scott's probably arrested and sequestered in a dimly lit interrogation room, he thought. Most likely Elmer would be charged with kidnapping. Maybe even evading the law. For sure, they'd throw the book at him for hoarding cleaning supplies.

The knot in his gut tightened. He needed a plan, a good one. But first, he needed to take care of the nosy police officer.

YOU DESERVE A BREAK TODAY

Sunday, March 15, 2020, 6:18 a.m.

At 12:23 a.m., the cruiser's tires squealed and the police car sped away.

Elmer waited until its siren faded, then walked down the hall and began banging on Trudy's door.

His explanation for waking his sister brought the type of wrath that can only be unleashed by a younger sister who's always resented her older brother for inheriting the home place. Trudy's summer of love in Haight-Ashbury had been the start of a hippy-dippy lifestyle that sealed the deal—and deed to the farm—in Elmer's favor.

Once he explained the urgency, she agreed to get dressed and move her rig. At the edge of the motel parking lot, he started a small fire in an empty space and hurried back to his room. From the window, he watched Trudy's truck with his cargo pull away.

Six hours later, Elmer awoke to find Jim trying to make his bed. Though tempted to explain that the motel had staff for that task, he found himself encouraged by Jim's recovery and pleasant demeanor. Gone were the groans and moans of the night before. He had dressed himself in Elmer's dungarees and sweatshirt. Sometimes a body needs to feel useful, Elmer thought, and dressing for the part helps.

"Feeling better?"

"I'm upright and moving," Jim answered. "At my age, that's all I can ask for."

Jim switched on the television and then turned the sound down.

"Any word from your sister about my phone? Or Scott?"

"You don't happen to know his number, do you?"

Jim shook his head. "It's saved in my contacts. I never have to dial it."

"I'm sure we'll figure out a way to get in touch with him."

He was convinced of no such thing. Elmer felt certain the boy had confessed to stealing Jim from the rehab facility and a long stint in a county jail was in Elmer's future.

"You must be one of those glass-half-full people," said Jim. "Any kids?"

"We tried. Didn't work out. Why do you ask?"

"Where there's money, the parent-child relationship gets tangled. Scott's a good boy. Responsible. Maybe too much so." He smoothed out wrinkles. "Scott needs to play more and work less. My daughter has the playing thing down all too well. Maybe after I'm gone, Scott will relax a little."

"Careful what you wish for," said Elmer. "Most times what we say about our health tends to happen."

"Good point. I was circling the drain in that death camp. I could tell from the questions my kids asked that they were already planning what to do with their inheritance."

"I have the opposite problem." Elmer finished trimming his beard and mustache and put the electric razor back in his Dopp kit. "I don't have anyone to leave the farm to."

"What about your sister?"

"Trudy? She'd turn it into a pot farm."

Elmer wiped down the sink and lip of the toilet, placed dirty towels by the door, and killed the bathroom light.

Pausing in front of the TV, he said, "I miss the days of Cronkite and Brinkley."

"And Huntley, Jennings, Reynolds, and Reasoner. Remember those nightly news death totals from the war? Boy, those were the days, huh?"

On the TV, a reporter said, "Financial analysts say yesterday's move by the Fed to reduce interest rates to zero shows no sign of stopping the sell-off on Wall Street."

"Zero interest rates," Elmer grumbled. "Like that's a good idea. Just ask Jimmy Carter."

"You vote for him?"

"Nicest president we ever had," Elmer answered. "Got dealt a bad hand. Sure, the Arab oil embargo caused oil prices to skyrocket, and that led to high inflation and a global recession, but Carter could have put pressure on the Fed sooner. Giving away money always comes back to bite."

On television, the network news co-host gave his take on the day's events.

"That's right, Miranda. In addition to the Fed's dramatic steps today to keep the economy from plunging into a recession or worse, first responders and hospitals are preparing for a massive influx of patients exhibiting serious symptoms."

"Serious symptoms, my foot," said Jim. "If they want to see serious, they ought to visit the death camp I escaped from."

"Yogurt and some fresh orange juice ought to perk you right up," Elmer said. "Though it's debatable how fresh the fruit is in a three-star motel like this."

The newscast switched to a video of a government health official standing on the steps of the U.S. Capitol. "The U.S. should plan for a worst-case pandemic. Our response should be a united effort with the kind of intense implementation that served us so well during World War II."

"World War II?" Elmer clicked off the set.

Making a final walk around the room, he checked to make sure they had not left anything that might point to their identities.

"Some people are sick, is all."

Elmer held the door for Jim, then made sure the door latched and locked.

"You serve?"

"Korea," said Jim. "You?"

With Elmer supporting Jim, the pair walked slowly down the hall. "Nam. Similar conflict with the same outcome. Our side gave up and went home. My sister protested the war. When I got back, she called me a baby killer."

"You two seem to get along okay now."

"Time heals all wounds," Elmer said.

Passing the elevator, Jim glanced out the large window that overlooked the pool and patio. "Could be an interesting travel day. A little rain, maybe."

"Rain I'm not worried about. It's snow and ice that gets my britches in a wad.'

Reaching the lobby, the pair found the breakfast bar closed due to COVID.

"Oh, for crying out loud. I'm going to speak to the desk clerk to see if he can make change for the vending machine."

"I'll hit the head one more time. At my age, I never pass up a chance to pee."

Elmer joined a short line of masked guests wishing to check out, his attention riveted on the lobby TV. A female news reporter ran down the morning's top news headlines.

"Some are saying Monday's opening could be the worst week in the history of Wall Street," the reporter said.

A couple dropped off their key card, complained loudly about there being no breakfast, and stormed out the front door.

"In the past seventy-two hours," the news reporter continued, "officials across Montana and the western states have moved to slow the spread of the coronavirus. Tribal governments have declared states of emergency, Yellowstone and Glacier National Park have restricted access, and Montana schools have shut down statewide. Bars and restaurants in major cities, including Billings and Missoula, have been ordered to close or switch to takeout only, while rural hospitals brace for potential outbreaks."

Wearing a collared shirt, slacks, and loafers, another guest placed his receipt on the counter and questioned an additional charge.

"Give me a break," said the woman in front of Elmer. "At this rate, I'll get charged an extra day before I check out."

"You could simply drop off your key," the man in front of her suggested.

"And get billed for something I didn't agree to?" the woman replied. "No way."

Trying to lighten the mood, Elmer asked, "Either of you ever watch Butch Cassidy and the Sundance Kid?"

"Sure. Why?" the man asked.

"'Cause it seems everyone's wearing masks. I'm trying to remember if they wore masks when they robbed that bank of Bolivia. I used to know these things."

"You're not," said the woman. "Wearing a mask, I mean."

Elmer reached into his hip pocket and placed his handkerchief over his mouth.

"No masks," the man said. "But Butch didn't know Spanish."

"You're up," the woman said to the man.

He placed his key card on the counter. "Butch and Sundance's girlfriend had to write down instructions for what to say."

"And then, in Spanish, Butch tried to tell the people in the bank to get their hands up and stand against the wall." Chuckling, Elmer said, "One of the funniest scenes in the movie."

Impersonating Sundance, the man said, "'They have their hands up! They're against the wall, already!'"

Still laughing, Elmer said, "They don't make movies like that anymore."

The man checked his receipt. "Looks good. Thanks." Walking past Elmer, he said, "'Keep thinking, Butch. That's what you're good at.'"

From outside, Trudy rushed in. "Let's go."

"We have to wait for Jim."

"Our ride's waiting. Come on."

"I can't—"

Trudy grabbed Elmer's elbow and yanked him out of line. "Now!"

Elmer followed her gaze toward the television, where the screen had switched to local news. "In Great Falls," the anchor was saying, "authorities are on the lookout for two individuals suspected of kidnapping."

A grainy picture of Trudy's rig and two enlarged bubblehead shots of Elmer and Trudy stepping from the cab filled the screen.

Trudy and Elmer made a mad dash for the door.

IT'S UNCONSCIONABLE WHAT PEOPLE DO IN A TIME OF CRISIS

Sunday, March 15, 2020, 6:26 a.m.

A wall of guests unloading from a shuttle blocked Trudy and Elmer's escape. Gym bags and jerseys announced that the Wyoming Weed Picker's Soccer Team had arrived. On the television, the newscast had switched to a doctor standing in front of a hospital with patients lying on stretchers.

"What is happening in our country is horrendous," said the doctor. "We have a dwindling supply of ventilators and cleaning supplies and hundreds more patients than we can handle. All we can do is declare defeat and try to save those we can. The young and those with the best chance of survival are being prioritized. "

Trudy leaned in close to Elmer, her voice barely above a whisper. "We need to get out of here before those soccer players recognize us."

"Not yet. We have to wait for Jim to get back."

Before Trudy could argue further, a woman with the word Coach on her warm-up suit said, "Hey, I know you two. You're the ones who snatched that old geezer from the nursing home."

"And they're smuggling a shipment of vital health supplies to Canada," said one of the players. "Look! They're on TV!"

"It's unconscionable what people will do in a time of crisis," said Great Falls, Channel 5 news anchor. "If you see these two, please report them immediately to authorities."

Once more, two enlarged bubblehead images of Elmer and Trudy filled the screen.

"The pair is wanted for human trafficking and by the Bureau of Land Management for hoarding much-needed medical cleaning supplies," said the news anchor. "They're considered dangerous. Do not approach."

Trudy pushed Elmer, forcing the pair through the scrum. "Go!"

"Oh, no you don't," said the coach, grabbing the back of Elmer's jacket. "You're staying right here until the police arrive."

Surrounded, Elmer scanned the lobby for a way out, then he saw it: the door to the patio. Grabbing Trudy's hand, he pulled her through the closed breakfast area and shoved her out the door leading to the outside pool. As he was about to exit, he caught sight of Jim waddling toward him.

Calling over his shoulder, Elmer yelled, "Meet us in the parking lot! Hurry! We'll pick you up!"

Shoving aside stacked lounge chairs, the pair slipped out the pool area's side gate and jogged around the building. Waving wildly, Trudy signaled to the driver of a yellow Kia sedan.

The Kia's passenger window rolled down. "You Trudy?" asked the driver.

"Yes." Trudy opened the passenger door and hopped in. Leaving the door open, she shouted to Elmer, "Backseat! Get in!"

"You request ride?"

"We have to wait for Jim," Elmer said.

"You need ride?" the driver asked.

"Yes, yes," Trudy answered. "Now let's go."

"What about Jim?" Elmer asked.

"Get in! We'll wait a few more seconds," Trudy answered.

Looking back, uncertain Jim would see them, Elmer climbed in. While he attempted to buckle his seatbelt, Trudy got out, slammed his door shut, and got back into the passenger seat.

The driver carefully placed his phone in its dashboard cradle and studied it as though it were a new constellation in the night sky. Finally, he said, "You still no tell where you go."

"We're waiting for a friend," Elmer said.

"The old man's time's up," said Trudy. "Just drive."

"But where go?" asked the driver.

Elmer looked out the back window and saw Jim shuffling toward them on the sidewalk. "Don't leave yet. Jim's coming."

"And he's bringing a crowd," Trudy replied, pointing. "Put this thing in gear and let's go!"

"No need for yell," the driver mumbled.

Elmer leaned over the front seat. "She's a might testy in the morning before she's had her coffee."

Glancing at the driver, she said, "You want to see testy? Keep asking 'Where go?'" Trudy put her hand on the shift lever and yanked it into drive. "Go!"

With the Kia speeding out of the motel parking lot, Elmer said, "Circle back to the lobby drop-off area. We have to pick up Jim."

"Keep driving," Trudy countered.

"Go back?" asked the driver.

"Yes," Elmer answered.

"Straight ahead!" screamed Trudy.

Just then, a white Ford pickup with a lime-green stripe down its side and a BLM Fire logo on its driver-side door passed them. Parking in the drop-off area, the Bureau man from land management stepped out and jogged inside the motel.

Looking at Elmer in his rearview mirror, the driver asked, "Circle back?"

"Guess not," Elmer answered.

"But I drive where?"

Trudy pointed out the front windshield and yelled, "Away from here!"

"DANGEROUS FUGITIVES" IS A BAD LOOK

Sunday, March 15, 2020, 6:27 a.m.

Trudy pulled out her phone. It was larger than the one Edith had owned. Large enough that—when he leaned over the front seat—Elmer could see his face and Trudy's above the words "Dangerous Fugitives" on the TV newscast.

"NO! I am NOT exaggerating, Chelsea," the male announcer was saying. "What you're seeing behind me is a motel where only minutes ago this pair of kidnappers released their hostage and carjacked a rideshare vehicle."

"This is worse than bonehead stupid," said Trudy. "You know how much time I could get if convicted of kidnapping?"

Elmer did not know and was not inclined to estimate. "This isn't as bad as it looks. We'll simply—"

Trudy cut him off. "There is no 'we.' There is no 'we'll.'" Trudy scanned the road ahead. "This is all your doing. You. YOU WILL FIX THIS."

"I still make payments," the Kia owner said. "This not safe."

Trudy, pointing at the traffic ahead, said, "Getting into a wreck won't help matters."

"I drive only by blue line. I need destination."

"Keep straight until I tell you to turn," said Trudy.

"But you have destination?"

"Yes," Trudy replied. "We have a destination. You driving away from that motel is our destination."

"I, um, sorry, but I cannot take you, um, until I know where you go. We have policy."

She pointed to a McDonald's at the next corner. "There, in that parking lot. Destination."

"McDonald's?" Elmer asked.

The driver swung the Kia into the parking lot and nosed in next to a handicapped space.

Trudy opened her door. "Elmer, you stay in the car."

Bolting toward the side door, she banged on its glass.

"She probably needs to use the women's room," Elmer said. "I went before I checked out. Always do. Last thing I take care of before—"

"You have app?"

Elmer considered his question. "I have a lucky rabbit's foot. It's gotten me out of a couple of jams. You have an app?"

"Oh, yes, sir, I have app. Our company develop app. All our drivers thoroughly trained to use app. I have cousin in Bombay, he work on development team. App say you need destination before blue line show."

Seeing his sister banging on the door's glass window and yelling, "Let me in!" Elmer replied, "You must be proud."

"Very, sir. Big honor for our family."

"And I bet your brother is proud of you."

"Oh, sir, most. I live in America and make most money than he."

Trudy returned, yanked open the driver's door, and pointed. "You. Out!"

"Um?"

Before he could protest, Trudy reached across him and unbuckled his safety belt.

"Out! Now!" Pointing to faint paint markings on the pavement, she said, "You parked too close to that handicapped space. The restaurant's manager needs to speak with you!"

"What manager? I no see manager."

"He's coming out the back door now. Look."

Appearing confused and embarrassed, the driver stepped from the car. "I ... I am not too near. There is much space."

Trudy slid behind the wheel of the Kia and, without waiting to buckle her seat belt, threw the vehicle into reverse and backed away.

"Wait! You no take my car!" yelled the driver.

Elmer asked from the back seat, "Are we stealing a car?"

"Borrowing."

"You mean like a library book?"

"Hush talking!" Trudy turned up the volume on the dashboard radio. "I want to hear what they're saying."

The radio announcer's somber words did little to relax the knot in Elmer's gut.

"This morning it was announced that the U.S. Capitol has canceled all tours," said the radio announcer. "In Florida, all Weeki Wachee mermaid shows are closed. In California, the Santa Monica Pier is closed. Closer to home, Montana's Bigfoot Discovery Museum, Nevada's Clown Motel, and Oregon's Vortex House of Mystery are shut down in response to the pandemic."

"Clever marketing," said Trudy, "Sliding in the Santa Monica Pier among the Capitol and Disney closings. What do you want to bet the pier is a sponsor of National Public News?"

"What I bet is that cops are already looking for a stolen Kia."

"Pay attention," Trudy replied. "You're going to need to know how to retrace this route."

"MGM Resorts in Las Vegas have shuttered all its casinos," the announcer continued. "And many, if not most, public schools across America, including New York, will be closed starting Monday."

Taking in the plowed snowbanks pushed to the edge of the streets, Elmer said, "Looks as if kids in Great Falls get plenty of snow days already."

A female news reporter broke in. "Chet, this is Miranda reporting from Times Square. Here in New York City and the boroughs, grocery stores are empty. Mayor Bill de Blasio announced that the city will restrict bars, restaurants, and cafes to takeout order deliveries only. He has said he will sign an executive order that calls for the closure of all city nightclubs, movie theatres, and concert venues. The mayor's restrictions are in line with other cities, like Washington, DC, and those in California. In Miami and Fort Lauderdale, the beaches are closed. With bars and restaurants shuttered, college students who flocked to Florida for spring break now find themselves wandering about the streets with no place to go."

"Closing beaches?" said Trudy. "What do they think these kids are going to do? Sit in their motel rooms and watch this steady stream of depressing news?"

Elmer asked, "What do you want to bet that before this is over, the suicide rate skyrockets?"

"Miranda, it's almost like we are witnessing a zombie apocalypse before our very eyes. I think Americans should resign themselves to hunkering down significantly more than we, as a country, are doing."

Trudy raced through yellow lights, sped down a service road that ran parallel to the interstate, then made a hard left into an industrial complex.

"To your point, Chet, the governor of California released an executive order that gives the state authority to take over hotels and motels to house potential coronavirus patients."

Speeding past empty parking spaces, Trudy reached a gated fence, navigated a tight U-turn, and threw the Kia into reverse.

"And yet even as poll workers are calling to say they can't or won't come in," said Chet, "Ohio, Illinois, Florida, and Arizona are still planning to hold their primaries Tuesday. All this with the elderly quarantined in their homes and college students unable to vote due to residency issues."

"I fear we are on the verge of our entire electoral process coming under attack," said reporter Miranda.

She pulled alongside the fencing so close Elmer couldn't open his door.

"My truck is inside there."

She turned off the car and handed Elmer the keys to the KIA.

"Driving through that gate'll mess up my rig's grill some, but I've done worse. Park this car three blocks from that McDonald's and walk there. Buy a biscuit or something. When they give you the order, turn so they don't see you, drop the keys in the bag, and then ask the cashier to run the meal over to our driver. Explain that you're buying a homeless person breakfast, but you want to remain anonymous. Leave before they can ask questions."

"And you think the car's owner won't see me?"

"Not if you hoof it out of there quick, no. I'll pick you up at that Exxon we passed. Don't dilly-dally. We're wanted fugitives, but the law might not have a good description of my rig."

Elmer said nothing. He'd spent the better part of his life reading the weather. Judging from Trudy's demeanor, a storm was brewing, and he wasn't about to risk getting zapped by a bolt of anger.

Elmer watched his sister climb onto the roof of the Kia, clamber over the fence, and drop down. Sprinting to her truck, she reached her rig seconds before a Doberman launched itself at the driver's door.

In all his years on the farm, Elmer had never been so relieved to hear the rat-a-tat-tat-tat-tat of a diesel engine coming to life.

Sliding into the driver's seat, he drove away in the Kia: parked on a side street, locked up, and started walking to the McDonald's.

Taking in the eerie silence of mostly empty streets, one thought came to him: If poll workers don't show up to verify votes, or if voters can't get to the polls, wouldn't it be easy for a losing candidate to claim voter fraud? He pictured a scenario with election results coming in, but with fewer votes counted than anticipated. If that happened, the legitimacy of the election might come into question. Elmer imagined accusations flying, protests erupting, and a government in disarray.

The Golden Arches came into view.

Also coming into view was a police car pulling up to the sidewalk next to him.

A LONG WAY TO GO, AND SHORT TIME TO GET THERE

Sunday, March15, 2020, 6:58 a.m.

Elmer kept his head down, ball cap pulled low over his eyes, and waited for the officer to jump out and arrest him. Instead, the driver flipped on the lights and siren and sped off toward the storage facility. That could only mean one thing—Trudy had busted down the gate.

Spying the Kia owner loitering outside the restaurant's padlocked playground, Elmer fell into a line behind a Chevrolet Suburban, making its way to the first drive-through window.

In front of the McDonald's, one police car sped past, then another.

While the Chevrolet Suburban's driver ordered, he tucked in close to its bumper. Right on his backside, a Ford F-450 Super Duty truck closed the distance, its engine heat making him feel like a rotisserie chicken. The Suburban's brake lights momentarily flashed off, and he shuffled forward, blending in with the vehicles.

When his turn arrived, Elmer ordered a sausage, egg, and cheese sandwich with hash browns and orange juice. At the next window, he received his bag of food and dropped the car keys inside. Asking to borrow a pen, he wrote down the street number where he'd parked the Kia and requested that the order be delivered to the man standing by the closed playground. Elmer then slipped the attendant a five dollar bill and walked away before the woman could refuse his favor.

Peering around the corner, he saw an officer chatting with the driver. Worse, he spotted Jim seated in the back of the police car. Overcome with regret and shame, Elmer walked beside the Ford

F-450 Super Duty truck, using it as cover, until he exited the parking lot and slipped out of sight.

Spying Trudy's rig at their meeting spot, Elmer jumped into the passenger seat.

Glaring at him, Trudy said, "Elmer, we're in deep trouble! That old guy we kidnapped isn't just an escapee from an assisted living facility. He's a former high-level scientist who worked on some classified projects with China. The NIH thinks he knows how COVID started!"

Elmer buckled his seat belt. "Jim? But he seemed so nice."

"The good spies always are. So now we're not only kidnappers. We're involved in a global conspiracy to create a pandemic. If we get caught, I might end up with a life sentence and you'll be on death row. We need a plan."

"Maybe we should turn ourselves in?"

Trudy gave him a withering look. "That's not a plan. That's your stupidity oozing out."

Giving the impression of thinking hard, Elmer rubbed his chin. "How about we wear disguises?"

Trudy glared. "Like, fake beards and mustaches? Have you lost your mind?"

Elmer fumbled with the road map. "I'll look for some alternate routes to Browning. Anything to keep us off the interstate."

She fiddled with the radio until a crackling news broadcast filled the truck.

"This is KGFM News with a breaking update on the fugitive case that is capturing regional attention. Local law enforcement, along with federal agents, are now in hot pursuit of two subversive saboteurs who allegedly kidnapped an elderly man from his home."

"That rehab facility wasn't his home," Elmer said.

"Like that matters now."

The announcer continued, "Civilians are urged to be on the lookout for these dangerous terrorists and not to approach them under any circumstances. The pair are believed to be armed and dangerous."

"Armed with what, hand sanitizer?"

"More troubling," continued the announcer, "the pair who may have been exposed to a new, more virulent strain of the virus. This makes these fugitives carriers of the disease, putting everyone they encounter at risk."

Trudy studied Elmer in stunned silence. "You and your great ideas."

Elmer rubbed his chin harder. With sirens from behind growing louder, Elmer said, "Maybe park this rig someplace where police helicopters can't spot it. You know, like among so many trucks, yours doesn't stand out."

"That's called a truck stop, dummy."

"You remember that movie *Smokey and the Bandit* we saw with that boy you were dating? I'm thinking that's our ticket out of this mess."

Trudy replied, "Are you suggesting we now steal a 1977 Pontiac Firebird Trans Am?"

"West bound and down, we're loaded up and truckin'. We goin' to do what they say can't be done. We've got a long way to go and a short time to get there."

"Elmer?"

"Yeah?"

"Stop singing."

"But you get what I'm saying, right?"

"Unfortunately… yes."

CLOSE THE DOORS AND THEY WALK AWAY

Sunday, March 15, 2020, 7:38 a.m.

Sighing louder than a truck tire losing air, Trudy snatched the CB mic like it owed her money. "Breaker, breaker, this is Snakebit. Any smokies heading north on one-five?"

"This is Big Red, Snakebit. You're clear for the next ten miles. Where you headed?"

"Browning, Big Red. Need to keep my nose clean."

"Roger that, Snakebit. We're rolling to Shelby. We can shield you if you'd like. We got five rigs and three more if need be."

"The more the better, Big Red. Where can I slide in?"

"We're coming past exit 278 right now, cruising at 65. You can merge in around mile marker 280."

"Copy that, Big Red. I'll look for you at 280. Thanks."

"Anytime, Snakebit. Keep it between the ditches."

Elmer hunched forward, scanning the road ahead and buildings on either side. "I probably ought to take a pee break before we hit the interstate."

"We've got a convoy to catch."

Pointing out the front window, Elmer said, "There, up ahead, there's a church. I'll run inside and use their bathroom."

"You don't even know if it's open."

"Almost eight on Sunday? Of course, it's open."

Downshifting, Trudy replied, "I don't see any cars in the parking lot, and they got orange cones blocking the entrance. What's that sign by their mailbox say?"

Squinting, Elmer read aloud, "Due to … COVID-19 … in-person services are paused. Join us online every Sunday at 10:00 a.m. for worship and then there's a string of letters I couldn't read. You sped by too fast."

"Guess you'll just have to be a big boy and hold it."

Elmer shifted uncomfortably in the passenger seat. "What sort of church closes on Sunday?"

Trudy shifted into gear and checked her mirrors. "You tell me." She spoke the church's name aloud, then handed her phone to Elmer. "What's it say on the church's webpage?"

Elmer hunched forward to read the screen on Trudy's Dick Tracy phone. "Nate Swanson is quoted as saying, 'We don't want to simply make it through this time of testing but to come out stronger and healthier as a church. We see COVID as a great opportunity to witness to the power of community.' Sounds more like a civic club than a church," said Elmer.

"I wouldn't know," Trudy replied. "I don't do church." Catching a green light, the truck accelerated through the intersection and gained speed as an interstate exit sign appeared ahead. "You?"

"Not since Edith died. Can't say as I miss it. Says here their church is acting in compliance with emergency government mandates. I'm betting they'll go broke and close if they keep people from coming to church." Elmer rested the phone on his thigh. "It's not like people are itching to give away their money. Way I see it, that tithing business is more like tipping the preacher and choir for a good performance."

"I got our convoy in sight," said Trudy. "Hang on, this is a tight turn."

Grabbing the armrest with one hand and the phone with the other, Elmer watched in amazement as his sister flawlessly shifted gear after gear. Seconds later, they reached cruising speed and were riding the bumper of a lime green Cooper Mini.

"A little close, aren't we?" Elmer said.

Trudy gave no ground, all but daring the driver of the Cooper to brake. Shifting into another gear, Trudy swung out past the Cooper with mere feet between Elmer and the driver.

Tipping his hat at the scowling driver, Elmer said, "Lady in that Matchbox car has more gray hair than you."

"And if she doesn't learn how to accelerate on an on-ramp, she won't make it to her next birthday. Is there more to the article?" Trudy asked.

"Guess not. The story stops mid-sentence."

"Swipe the screen."

"Swipe who?"

"With your finger," said Trudy. "Touch the screen and move it."

Quietly pleased to learn his finger had magical power, Elmer said, "The pastor is saying that weekends will look a lot different without people in the pews. I bet they will. Empty isn't a look most churches want. He goes on to mention something about video streaming and small group interaction being the key to keeping folk connected. I guess he means everyone using one of them phones like this because in the picture his Dick Tracy phone is facing the camera."

"I could explain how a smartphone works," Trudy said, "but I doubt you'd understand."

"I am certain I would not care. He says that he's hoping folk can remember that church is not a building but people. Man has faith. I'll give him that," Elmer continued. "But you just watch. Once government officials find they can shut down a church because a few people get a cold, they will shut down churches for other things, like not paying taxes. This country is broker than Job. Edith loved telling me how he had it all and lost it in a day."

"Why would she find that a fun fact?"

"Wanted to remind me to never rest on my backside. Like Mom and Dad didn't raise us right."

Hitting her blinker, Trudy merged right between a Peterbilt hauling logs and a rig transporting new BMWs.

"Finally…" In one of those rare moments, Trudy smiled. "Back among my people." Grabbing the mic, she said, "Big Red, thanks for the escort. If you see anything up ahead, give me a shout."

"Roger that, Snakebit."

Elmer said, "Meant to ask you, how'd you get this rig in that storage facility?"

"I keep a pair of opera binocs in the cab. I parked in the parking lot of a medical building, walked to the storage lot, and hid in the bushes until someone came out."

"At that hour?"

"A paneled van, no windows. You'd be surprised what people do in those units late into the night."

Quickly glancing over at Elmer, Trudy said, "You know, brother, you just might make this delivery after all."

"Never doubted for a moment. I knew you'd come through."

"You sure 'bout that?"

"Okay, maybe a little."

Approaching a Dynamic Message Sign, Elmer read silently:

AMBER ALERT
JAMES NEEDHAM HALL, 83
ABDUCTED IN BUFFALO, WY
LAST SEEN IN 1978 WHITE FREIGHTLINER CAB
WITH A RED TRAILER, LICENSE PLATE: WXY-1234
CALL 911 IF SEEN

Elmer frowned. "That's us, right?"

"You and your bonehead, dumb ideas."

RAINEY DAYS AND SUNDAYS ALWAYS GET ME DOWN

Sunday, March 15, 2020, 4:09 a.m.

A short way after passing under the Amber Alert, light rain began to fall. Quickly, it turned to snow flurries. Trudy kept her rig tucked tight in the convoy, complaining to Elmer about how they should have never agreed to help the old guy.

"Jim," Elmer said. "And he's only a few years older than me."

As if straining to keep from bursting a blood vessel in her furrowed forehead, she said slowly, "Old … guy… who … will … be … the … reason … you ... rot … in … prison."

With the passing of the snow shower, the pair settled into a strained silence that did little to loosen the tight knot in Elmer's gut.

"Some whiteout," said Elmer, trying to break the tension.

"I'm not complaining," Trudy replied.

"Me neither."

"Sounded like it. Sounded like rainy, snowy days and Sundays get you down."

"Boy, do I miss her."

"Edith?"

"Karen Carpenter." Elmer leaned back in his seat and closed his eyes. "Going to take a short snooze. Wake me if something comes up."

"Like blue lights?" Trudy asked.

"Or Browning."

Trudy downshifted.

The truck's loud air brakes jolted Elmer awake. As they approached the city limits of Browning, Montana, he glanced at Trudy, then looked out her window. The endless flat landscape abruptly gave way to a mountain range west of the town.

Feeling a bit melancholic, he took it all in. "All the years I ran that farm, I never felt like it was mine," he said. "Edith used to say our place was borrowed."

Trudy raised an eyebrow. "But you're debt free, so there's that."

"Money's not the point," he said, absently rapping a knuckle against the window's glass. "I mean, sure, it's great to have the place paid off, but who am I going to leave the place to? Not you."

"And why not?"

"You know better, Sis. You hated the farm."

"I'll lease it out. Let someone else manage it."

"I'm not leaving the land to you. I've put too many years of hard work into that place."

"And Edith," said Trudy. "Don't forget, she did her fair share and then some."

Lost in his thoughts, the ache he felt at thinking of Edith left Elmer humming, "Rainy Days and Mondays."

"What's with the solemn mood?" Trudy asked. "I would have expected that us reaching Browning without getting arrested for kidnapping, carjacking, or transporting highly valued cleaning supplies would have left you ecstatic."

He bent forward and made an effort to see the sun through clouds over Red Mountain.

"A little snow, then sleet and rain," said Elmer. "I guess I'm missing Dad."

"Because you loved clearing snow off our long drive?"

"With the plow on his tractor, yes. Also, the last time I was in Browning, the two of us shared a motel room."

"You and Dad? When?"

"My last summer of baseball," Elmer answered. "I was on that travel team, and we played a tournament on the reservation against the Browning Bobcats. Got our butts whipped, of course. Whole team, every one of them, could run faster than Paul Shaw, and he was the fastest kid on our team. Paul went on to run track for our high school and got a college scholarship."

Trudy came to a full stop at an intersection to allow a man on a horse to pass in front. "You have an address for where you want to drop off your load?"

With the back of his knuckles, Elmer rubbed bristles on his chin. Though he'd only been there one time, Browning seemed smaller than he remembered.

Avoiding the question, he replied, "What's that lady announcer saying about Montana?"

Turning up the volume on the radio, Trudy said, "Nothing good, I'm sure."

"This is Meredith Dylan of KBBZ news. Today we learned that, due to COVID-19, Logjam Presents, Montana's largest entertainment and production company, announced Saturday it will postpone all live events in Bozeman for the next thirty days. And although there have been no confirmed cases of COVID-19 in the Flathead Valley area, Big Sky and Whitefish Mountain resorts and Bridger Bowl Ski Area announced they would end the ski season prematurely due to COVID-19."

"Them radio people must be getting paid to say 'COVID-19.' It's like that's all they want to talk about," Elmer said.

"I keep telling you, this is bigger than you think. Only reason you don't know is because you live in a part of the world technology hasn't reached yet. There are tribes in the Amazon more plugged in than you."

"I know enough. I just choose not to give bad news the time of day."

"You'll give it the time of day when you're sick and on a ventilator."

"Doubt that I will, sis. Doubt I'll even give it a second thought."

"You miss Edith that much?"

"If you lost your better half, wouldn't you?"

"I'm divorced. My perspective is jaded."

Elmer tapped the radio's dash speaker. "Hush, so I can hear this."

"Red Lodge Mountain is suspending operations for a week and Target," Meredith Dylan continued, "and Rosauers in Missoula have started limiting the number of face and baby wipes, hand sanitizer, paper towels, and Lysol products customers can buy. Toilet paper is restricted to four rolls per customer."

"Shame you didn't stock up on TP," said Trudy, with a hint of sarcasm.

"I snagged a roll at the motel. You?"

"Both rolls."

Elmer pointed out the windshield. "Keep straight at the four-way stop sign. Then pull off at the edge of that field. I need to see if I can find someone at the tribal office to speak with."

"The Montana Department of Corrections has suspended visitation," Dylan was saying, "and the Montana Supreme Court will use video and telephone conferencing to hear cases and report verdicts."

"Maybe with courts scaling back," said Trudy, "our cases won't come to trial until we've expired."

"Speak for yourself," Elmer replied. "Soon as I'm done here, I'm heading to Bolivia."

"But didn't Butch and Sundance die in Bolivia?"

"We all got to go sometime."

"Rainy days and Sundays, Brother. They always get you down."

Stepping out of the truck, Elmer tugged the bill of his ball cap down over his brows and walked toward a long, single-story building that served as Browning's main strip shopping center. Beyond, the Livingston Range of Glacier National Park shielded the dim glow of a sun setting behind thick clouds. Nervous about how to bring up the matter, Elmer approached the front door of the Blackfeet Nation Tribal Administration Office. He knocked, then stepped to one side and peered through the front glass.

With her window rolled down, Trudy asked, "Well?"

"Well?" was Trudy's way of letting Elmer know she expected something more from the end of their great journey than a street with clapboard homes and abandoned vehicles parked on dirt drives.

"Looks like they're closed."

"It is a Sunday," Trudy replied.

"I mean like permanently." Hands cupped over his brow, he called back, "Boxes on tables and chairs stacked."

With mild disappointment at the desolation and poverty of the reservation, Elmer looked back down the street they'd traveled. "No choice but to find a place for the night."

Trudy asked, "You see anything that looked promising on our drive? 'Cause I sure didn't."

A rattling pickup approached from the direction of the range. With a wave of his hand, Elmer flagged down the truck's driver and started walking toward the vehicle.

When the driver rolled down his window, Elmer asked, "Which way to Glacier View?"

"If you're the gambling type, you might be about to come up snake eyes. There's talk the resort might close because of some sickness."

"But they're still open?" Elmer asked.

Half an hour later, Trudy and Elmer strolled into the Glacier View Hotel and Casino.

"I'm hitting the slots."

"I'm hitting the head," Elmer replied.

BETTING BIG ON THE FUTURE

Sunday, March 15, 2020, 6:18 p.m.

For a Sunday evening in March, the casino looked nearly deserted.

"It's COVID," the salesclerk explained. "That's why we're so empty. We've been getting reservation cancellations all day."

As if they were doing some shady back alley deal, the gift store employee slid Elmer a chocolate bar and then gave him his change.

"You have a mask? We're not supposed to let you stay on the property without one. We will, of course. We're not stupid. But Governor Bullock wants everyone to wear a mask inside. It's okay to eat in the casino, but you need to do it with a mask."

"No mask," Elmer said.

"Well ..." The salesclerk handed him the receipt. "That's our mask policy. Enjoy your candy and slots."

Amidst the thick fog of cigarette smoke that could've doubled as a weather system, Elmer spotted Trudy. He handed her the candy bar and made his way to the elevators. The doors opened and a couple, masked up, stepped out.

The woman's eyes narrowed at Elmer. "They sell these in the store." She tapped her mask. "It's a good idea to get a pack."

The man with her rolled his eyes in a way that suggested he'd been through this lecture more times than he cared to count.

"I feel fine. Haven't been sick since in forever."

"The mask isn't for you. You could have COVID and not even know until days later."

Elmer and the man exchanged glances. For a moment, Elmer thought he'd found an ally in this conversation.

"She's right, you know," the man said, extinguishing any hope of male solidarity. "They say you could be contagious three—"

"Five days," the woman interrupted. "Before symptoms appear."

Before Elmer could say more, the couple bolted.

Standing in the nearly empty casino, Elmer processed the whirlwind of recent events and how things had gone sideways. Helping Jim escape the assisted living facility had given Elmer a brief sense of pride and purpose, but the carjacking incident bothered him. Except for a pack of gum at age nine, he had never stolen anything. Now, because of their cross-country Lysol-smuggling operation, he and Trudy were considered wanted and dangerous fugitives.

Standing in an almost deserted casino on an Indian reservation, he hoped to put the cases of Lysol behind him and get back to living his normal, boring life.

The small crowd in the casino shoved quarters into slot machines and yanked handles. From a row of machines came the electronic *boop-boop-boop* the slots made when a machine paid out, and the clank of quarters landing in trays.

Elmer placed a card key on top of the machine. "Your room is across the hall from mine."

Trudy yanked the handle hard like she was trying to rip the machine's arm off.

"I'm going to see what's on the menu at the restaurant," Elmer continued.

The hostess seated Elmer as far from the bar as possible. The Glacier View Casino Café was one of those places where you can still feel the heat of the deep fryer and get a secondhand nicotine buzz without leaving your seat. Elmer had a pretty good idea his food would taste like a Marlboro, with a side of regret. Not that he was in any rush to chow down.

Something gnawed at his gut, and that gnawing had to do with a bank of TVs mounted behind the bar. On the screen directly in front of Elmer, a talking head yammered on about the sickness that was bringing all global commerce to a halt.

"The federal government, state and local officials, are asking private businesses across the state to consider aggressive voluntary closings. They are making it clear that if you don't voluntarily cooperate, they'll voluntarily make it mandatory. Spiking U.S. coronavirus cases could force rationing—yes, rationing—But this is not the time to panic. I repeat, this is not a time to panic and hoard vital essentials."

"Unless you need toilet paper," joked the talking head's co-host.

Elmer's waitress handed him a menu. "Can I get you something to drink? Beer? Wine? Cocktail?"

"Water."

"Our special this evening is whatever is left in the kitchen. We didn't get any food deliveries today, so the pickings are slim. I'll be right back with your water."

"Also, in a totally expected move," the male talking head continued, "a guy in Kentucky is now under police guard because he thought 'quarantine' was, like deodorant in an elevator, optional. Some people simply have no consideration for those around them. Sensible Americans simply will not tolerate you spewing your sickness on everyone around you. It's time for the president to mobilize the military to help fight this virus. Maybe a little martial law and order and military troops will get the attention of those who think 'quarantine' is a joke. This is only my opinion, of course, but I served as legal counsel for President Bill Clinton, so I know a thing or two about how to deal with national emergencies."

Elmer was not 100 percent sure how the military could fight a virus. He also wasn't 100 percent sure the guy on TV was, legally speaking, in his right mind. He had the wide-eyed look of someone on the verge of walking off the set.

"In Italy, residents can only set foot outside due to an urgent need, like buying necessities," Clinton's former legal counsel was saying. "And they are expected to carry a form justifying the reason for travel. Those in violation face the threat of a $235 fine for breaking the rules and possibly three months in prison. Italy isn't messing around. You yahoos who think this is a joke should get a clue. The coronavirus outbreak will also impact a long-running ideological confrontation within the United Methodist Conference over the issues of same-sex marriage and ordination of openly …"

Elmer's waitress arrived. He ordered broccoli soup and toast—bread and warmed-up soup being two of the few items remaining in the kitchen.

He was about to turn his attention back to the TV when a voice behind him asked, "That seat taken?"

Before Elmer could answer, a guy eased past and sat across from him in the booth.

Taking one of Elmer's two packs of crackers, he said, "Couldn't help but notice you're eating alone."

The man looked like he'd been carved out of granite, with shoulders that stretched the limits of his leather jacket.

Munching a Saltine, he said, "Word is, you might be sitting on something ... in … ah… demand." Leaning in, he closed the space between them. "I might be interested in that something."

Elmer offered his other pack of crackers.

The man ripped open the package, then glanced about the restaurant as if making sure no one was listening. "There are … um… people on the lookout for… well ... certain necessities you might think would be on store shelves, but are not. And these … ah… people would be inclined to, perhaps, without much provocation, take delivery of those items."

Elmer shifted nervously in his seat. "Maybe you've got the wrong guy."

The man chuckled. "Don't think so. That rig you rode in on … ah … one of my crew ran the tags. Turns out there's an amber alert and the laws looking for that trailer." The man's smile widened. "And the people in it."

Shifting his gaze, Elmer glanced toward the kitchen door next to the bar.

"She's coming with your soup," the guy said. "We simply need to finish our business first. I'm willing to make this easy for you. No need for paperwork, no formalities."

Elmer forced a weak smile. "Right. Easy is always better."

"See? I knew we'd get along just fine." The man stood. "Enjoy your soup. I'll be on the casino floor helping your sister get lucky at slots. But don't take too long. Good luck can go bad when you least expect it."

The waitress returned with his soup. Elmer tried to enjoy his meal, but the evening had lost its flavor, as had the vegetable broth.

"Life has a funny way of weighing us down with things," Edith used to tell him. "Wealth, worries, work, and stuff we don't need." Elmer had been holding on to a lot lately—and not simply the Lysol stored in the back of Trudy's trailer.

He sopped the remainder of the soup with the last morsel of his toast and, dabbing his lips with a napkin, left a folded five-dollar bill under the edge of his plate.

Outside in the chill of the night, he walked in the direction of a field of wigwams.

Once, years ago, he and his father had sat in one of those wigwams, talking. For Elmer, that night hadn't been about baseball, but the culture and history of a people left behind by progress. If still alive, Little Feet, their team's star left-handed pitcher, would be easy to recognize. Any ball player missing his right arm was.

ELMER'S BIG BET

Monday, March 16, 2020, 7:04 a.m

A little after seven the next morning, Trudy banged on Elmer's door. When he opened it and peered out, his sister showed Elmer the screen on her phone.

"What am I looking at?"

Trudy replied, "It's a text message for you. Did you give someone my number?"

"Well, I don't have a phone, so yeah. My reading glasses are on the bedside table. What's it say?"

"That the council is meeting at nine this morning to discuss your offer."

"Those jumbled letters say all that?"

"I'm reading between the lines." She shoved the phone in her hip pocket. "Don't give out my number again."

"Do what?"

"Give my number to strange men."

"The Blackfeet are not strange," Elmer said. "They're normal folk. How'd you make out on the slots?"

"Better than I expected. We still checking out at eleven like planned?"

"If all goes well."

"Then I'll put my stuff in the cab. Look for me on the casino floor."

Dark clouds and whipping wind promised snow. The sooner he and Trudy got on the road, the better. Four construction trailers stood where a field of wigwams once formed a circle. Only five remained, rebuilt for tourists seeking a "Blackfeet Experience."

Mounting the steps of a trailer marked "Office," he knocked and entered.

The tribal leaders sat around a long table. Along one wall, through windows that looked west, low, gray clouds obscured mountain peaks.

The Blackfeet Nation Tribal Leader, an older man with silver hair flowing off his shoulders and wearing a black button-down dress shirt and jeans, leaned forward to rest an elbow on the conference room table. "How."

Elmer studied the man, unsure if he should dare answer.

"How!" repeated the leader.

Elmer chanced a response. "Now Brown Cow?"

Though trying to keep his expression stern, a faint smile betrayed the tribal leader. "Old you are, Fudd."

Fudd… As in Elmer Fudd. He hadn't heard that since his baseball days.

"As are you, my old friend." Elmer made a slow appraisal of the assembly. "Is this all the Council? I thought there'd be more members."

"Attrition and apathy. Our youth are no longer interested in our customs."

"Same here," Elmer replied. "Education was supposed to help 'em get ahead, but all it's done is bury 'em in debt with student loans."

"Ours learn how our land and culture were stripped away," the leader said. "They see the white man as an occupier."

"For kids in Kansas, the good life feels out of reach," Elmer said. "Salaries lag. Rent climbs. Many look elsewhere for answers."

"Perhaps they should spend time on our reservation to see what living at the mercy of the government is like. Through broken treaties, forced relocations, and government policies, our people have been marginalized and their nomadic lifestyle with its vast freedom destroyed."

"That's why I'm here," Elmer said. "I'm hoping to make right some of the past wrongs."

"How so?"

"I have a proposition. May I?"

At the tribal leader's gesture, Elmer took his place at the end of the table opposite his boyhood nemesis and laid out his grand plan. The Council listened intently, their expressions fixed in a stoic manner that made reading the room impossible.

Concluding, Elmer asked, "So? What'd you think?"

"To be clear," said Little Feet, "you are deeding all the assets listed on this trucking manifest to Blackfeet Nation? Plus the cases of hand wipes, sanitizer, and disinfectant you have in storage at Cut Bank?"

"Yes, but we have to move fast. There's another interested party and the sooner the items are out of my possession, the safer for me and my sister."

"Pauly D's guy," the tribal leader said. "The Outfit wants our casino. They see reservations as untapped ground."

"The way he talked, the house felt rigged."

"All bets are legit and on the up and up. His people handle our logistical needs. Getting supplies to the rez can be difficult at times. Parts, food, building materials ... but we keep Pauly D's people far from the money side of things."

"And here I was thinking the mob didn't exist anymore."

"Like us, they are a shell of what they once were," Little Feet said. "But they're still around, and because they need more ways to wash money, they want to take over."

A member of the council chimed in. "The items in Cut Bank—how much?"

"Yes," Elmer said. "I planned a second barn before Edith got sick. Frugal Storage in Cut Bank gave me the best rate, and I paid three years upfront. It's all on the manifest. Yours to keep."

"What will you tell Pauly D's man?

"What he wants to hear—meet me at Frugal Storage for the exchange."

"A gamble. Won't he wonder where the goods went when you show up empty?"

"I'm working on that. Do we have a deal?"

All five council members nodded.

"Let the chips fall," Little Feet said.

ELMER'S BIG BET, BAIT, AND SWITCH

Monday, March 16, 2020, 8:17 a.m.

Trudy pulled the truck to a stop near a long, single-story warehouse on the Blackfeet Nation reservation.

"This… is the place?" Killing the engine, she glanced at Elmer. "Doesn't look like much of a storage building."

"Poverty is the ex who keeps finding a way to make your life miserable," Elmer said. "Let's unload and skedaddle."

Trudy checked her side mirrors. "You sure that mobster guy ain't around? He could have tailed us. He could be out there, hiding, waiting for us to slip up."

"He's back at the casino, on the floor, making his rounds. I made sure of it."

"But how'd you get him to agree to meet in Cut Bank?" Trudy asked.

"Told him I had the Lysol—and some other items—stashed in a storage unit, and we'd have to meet up this afternoon. But I dropped a hint, you know, made it sound like I was looking for something bigger than just the cash. Got him thinking maybe there was a bigger score in it for him."

"So you let him think he could double-cross you and get more? Smart move. Or incredibly dumb."

Elmer climbed out of the truck and waved to the Blackfeet crew sent to help unload.

"He was going to try, anyway. That's what cons do. I simply fed him what he wanted to hear. Dangled just enough bait to make him bite."

"Well, let's unload and get back on the road before he figures out you're stringing him along."

The pair sent to help looked like they'd been cast for a Quenton Tortellini film. Twins—brother and sister—were built like they could bench-press the truck.

Elmer kept checking back across the field and up the road, his unease growing with each box they unloaded. The longer they stuck around, the greater the odds something could go wrong.

"Maybe this will help make things right with Edith."

Elmer shot Trudy a hard look. "How'd you know what I was thinking?"

"You're a short read, Brother, and not all that interesting. Still, say this whole trip was one huge, bonehead stupid move."

"Thanks for reminding me that my best isn't good enough, Sis."

With the truck unloaded, the male twin approached with the paperwork. "Sign here and here. Initial there." Another page flipped. "And initial here, here, sign here and there, and here."

Elmer scowled. "Lot of paperwork for me giving you free stuff."

"If there's one thing we learned from the white man, it's the importance of signed agreements."

Elmer handed over the signed papers, giving ownership to the Nation.

"You're making some serious enemies doing this," the young man's sister said.

His voice, almost a whisper, Elmer replied, "I owed this to your people. Or at least to Little Feet. My last at bat, he served up a pitch I could hit. We were getting waxed, and he didn't want me to go hitless in the tournament."

"He's that way—always honoring those who show honor." The boy hung the clipboard on a nail next to the rolling door. "It's officially transferred. Sister, let's ride!"

Mounting horses without saddles, the pair rode off like a group of young braves about to confront Custer, leaving Elmer to wonder if they were heading into a storm or just running away from one. And then . . .

THE GREAT CUT BANK CHASE

Monday, March 16, 2020, 8:43 a.m.

With the last empty corrugated container loaded in the trailer, Trudy asked, "What's your plan for when Pauly D's guy catches on that you've sold him a truckload of empty Lysol boxes?"

Elmer shrugged. "We get him looking the wrong way while we go the other."

Trudy's grin widened. "Ah, the classic egg… straction. Like when we convinced Mr. Johnson his chickens had flown the coop."

"And you told him they'd scrambled right over the fence."

"He didn't think that was funny," said Trudy, chuckling. "But while he was out there searching every bush and ditch, we gathered those eggs and hightailed it out of the henhouse. Remind me, how much did we make off that caper?"

"Enough for handlebar tassels for our Spyder bikes."

"Egg… cept this time, it's not some old farmer we're dealing with." Trudy opened the door to her cab and stepped on the running board. "Better hope this mob guy is as dumb as Mr. Johnson."

Elmer had doubts about that part. His big bet and switch reminded him of the time he'd dressed up as a bank robber for Halloween, borrowed his neighbor's riding lawnmower for a joyride, and ended up mowing over the mayor's mums. When finally cornered in a cul-de-sac and caught—and because he looked like a hoodlum—the arresting officer threatened to charge him with grand larceny, willful destruction of public property, disturbing the peace of parents out trick-or-treating with their kids, operating a vehicle without a license, impersonating a horticulturist, reckless endangerment of children, and fleeing the scene of a crime. At age nine, what he'd thought was harmless mischief had scared him straight.

Never again did he steal a riding lawn mower.

His big bet and switch had the same mix of dread and excitement. He had planned everything down to the last detail. But then again, he had also planned his last fishing trip down to the last detail, which ended with him losing two rods, a cooler, and his pants in the lake.

Still thinking about fishing and lawn mowers, Elmer stepped into the cab.

Trudy slammed her driver's door shut and the low rumble of an engine coming to life gave his heart a start. Looking back toward Browning's city limits, he spotted a black Dodge Charger speeding toward them.

Trudy shifted into first gear and asked, "Like old times?"

"Only maybe faster than we left Mr. Johnson's chicken coop. I think that's Pauly D's guy speeding toward us."

Trudy pulled the truck onto the highway and drove east, racing through the gears.

Looking in his side-view mirror, he saw the black Charger loom larger.

"He's onto us, isn't he?" Gripping the shift knob, Trudy's knuckles whitening, she frantically tried to coax more speed from the truck. "You and your bonehead—"

"He thinks he's got us," Elmer interrupted. "But we'll show him. He has no idea who he's messing with."

"Oh, I think he knows exactly who he's messing with, and he's not worried at all."

Elmer kept his eyes on the road ahead, but the tightness in his chest grew heavier with each white divided line that blurred past.

Trudy asked, "Has it occurred to you that the feds and law and whoever else you think is going to bail you out of this fix might not show?"

"They'll show."

"Your confidence in the government is admirable, Brother. I've always loved that child-like optimism of yours."

"You watch. This is going to be a big score for the feds."

Trudy shot a look at her side-view mirror, then back at the road. "Can't see the Charger. He must be nosed up close to the back bumper."

"Find out. Tap the breaks."

Trudy replied, "And have him crash into my trailer?"

"I'll pay for the repairs."

"Dog on right you will." Trudy stomped the brakes, then let off. "Ha! He's spinning crossways in the middle of the road. That'll show him."

Elmer checked his mirror. The Charger's driver regained control, stopped momentarily, and then peeled away, burning rubber.

"Didn't shake him," Elmer said. "We need a better plan."

Out the front windshield, orange barrels from a construction zone appeared, diverting traffic into the oncoming lane.

Downshifting, Trudy said, "The gig's up, Brother. End of the road for us."

"Run over those cones," Elmer said. "Smash'em."

"Why would I do that?"

"Remember the time Old Man Harper's cattle took over Main Street?" Elmer asked.

As they approached the line of orange barrels, the rig slowed.

"We tied a bunch of tin cans to the cows' tails," Trudy replied, "and started a stampede."

"And by the time Harper caught his cows, we were long gone."

Trudy downshifted, the engine growling. "Ended up with cows and cans scattered all across the road," she said.

"Now you're getting the idea."

Elmer checked his mirror and spotted the charger alongside the truck.

"Cows or cans or cones, I don't care which it is. But you better do something to shake that guy. He's waving a handgun out the window."

"Fine. Here goes."

She yanked the air-horn cord, producing a deafening blast. Instead of moving over, Trudy steered straight for the merge point, splitting the lanes. Dropping his flag, the road crewman sprinted toward the shoulder and jumped into the ditch. With a series of loud thuds, the truck plowed into the barrels, scattering them across the highway.

Elmer looked in the side-view mirror just in time to see the Charger slam into the bouncing barrels.

"Ha! He's in the ditch, nose down," said Trudy. She brought her rig to a stop. "He'll be stuck there for a while."

Elmer exhaled, but his relief was short-lived. "Guess we'll have to add endangering a work-zone employee to our list of charges."

A few minutes later, after a brief but heated chat with the road crew supervisor, they were back in line and clearing the work zone.

Trudy reached for the radio knob. "A little news to take your mind off Pauly D's guy?"

"Like the news ever leaves you feeling better," Elmer answered.

"Good morning. This is Mountain Public Radio, and I'm Wendy Toadonaburger with the latest on how our communities are responding to COVID-19. But first, in local news, attention is centered on the state of Montana and the Blackfeet Nation. An anonymous donation of Lysol products gifted to the tribe has become the focus of an investigation. Authorities, including the FBI and local officials, are on the lookout for a truckload of supplies linked to organized crime. The truck's driver and passenger are being pursued by officials on allegations of kidnapping and carjacking."

Elmer shifted in his seat, squinting at the side-view mirror. No sign of the Charger. Still, he couldn't shake the feeling that Pauly D's guy would reappear any second. From watching *The Godfather*, Elmer knew that revenge is a dish best served cold and Montana in March 2020 had the chill of a prolonged winter deep freeze.

THE GREAT CUT BANK CAPER

Monday, March 16, 9:39 a.m.

Trudy turned the volume down on the cab's radio. "See anything?"

Elmer craned his neck to check the mirror again. His gut grumbled. With breakfast skipped, lunch called. "Nothing yet."

On the radio, Wendy Toadonaburger droned on. "While details of the investigation remain limited, sources indicate that the Blackfeet Nation may be harboring fugitives who possess much-needed disinfectant supplies essential to preventing the spread of COVID-19. In other news, Montana businesses, including local storage facilities and distribution centers, have been inadvertently caught in the middle of this unfolding drama, with many rushing to rent units to house goods purchased in bulk."

Driving past the Welcome to Cut Bank sign, Trudy said, "For someone who spends his days doing pretty much nothing on a farm, you've turned this little delivery into a high-stakes, action movie."

"Couldn't be helped."

"Not true. You could have let the bureau man have the Lysol."

"And disappointed Edith?" Elmer turned up the radio. "I want to hear what this woman is saying."

"Several counties across Montana, including Missoula, Gallatin, Silver Bow, and Yellowstone, have taken decisive action to limit gatherings and slow the spread of the virus. This move comes in anticipation of St. Patrick's Day celebrations, a major concern for officials trying to prevent large crowds in downtown Missoula. Local health officer Ellen Leahy announced that all bars, restaurants, and gyms would close their doors, allowing only takeout, drive-through, and delivery services."

"Frugal Storage?" Trudy asked.

Elmer tried to make sense of the wording on its sign. Text: #FrugalOpen2477DaysAWeek.

"Best deal I could find this side of the rez. Looked more impressive in the brochure they mailed me."

Trudy pulled to the curb, partially blocking the eastbound lane running through Cut Bank.

"In Bozeman," Toadonaburger continued, "Gallatin County health officer Matt Kelley is urging to avoid gatherings of more than fifty people. Kelley, along with officials from other counties like Silver Bow's Karen Sullivan and Yellowstone's John Felton, emphasized the importance of social distancing, frequent handwashing, and staying home if feeling unwell. 'These health directives are essential to protecting the public and reducing strain on local healthcare systems.' Kelly said."

"Better go see if this code they gave me works," said Elmer.

"You've really never been here?"

Elmer opened his door and pivoted to step out. "Only jotted down this code and address and unit number and left it on the porch for the OneStopShop driver. When the boxes stopped arriving, I figured he either passed along this new address or kept the goods himself. Reckon I'll find out which, now."

At the metal gate, he keyed in the code. Based on the narrow alley access running south from the highway, maneuvering an eighteen-wheeler in and then backing it out would add to his sister's list of Things That Ruin My Day. The lift jack Trudy had stored in the trailer would have to do.

Working quickly, they soon had the truck fully unloaded, filling the unit with empty boxes marked Lysol Disinfectant Spray - Crisp Linen Scent.

Trudy checked her fancy Dick Tracy watch, the one she kept speaking into. "Twenty-two minutes. Faster than I'd expected."

"Desperation drives a man."

"And his sister."

"Amen to that. Now let's seal the deal so the feds have no reason to keep looking for us."

Trudy opened the top boxes of each of the first few pallets. "You better make sure I get all this money back."

"You will," Elmer said. "I promise."

Stacking bricks of cash inside, she then resealed the flaps with a hot-glue gun. "I worked too hard for this small fortune to see it sent to some evidence storage room."

"Pulling a one-arm-bandit isn't working," Elmer replied. "It's a fast way to go broke."

"Worked well enough for me."

"If Pauly D's guy hadn't rigged the slots for you, we wouldn't have any cash to use for bait."

"Still, what's mine is mine." Trudy wiped her hands on her jeans. "Lock it up?"

Elmer lifted a gym bag he'd carried from the cab and tossed it onto the pallet nearest the roll-up door.

"Copies of all Edith's past OneStopShop orders?" Trudy asked.

"Receipts, documents, cash, names—enough to tie Pauly D's guy to everything the Chicago Outfit is doing behind the scenes at the casino."

"But won't this put a crimp in your tribal friends' casino operation?"

"The Council will find another group to take over. Rez gambling work is profitable work."

"How'd you manage to get your hands on so much incriminating evidence?"

"Funny thing about hiring locals. In the mob's case, you can pay them to work, but that's not the same as buying loyalty. Little Feet spread the word about what I needed and suddenly envelopes and paper bags showed up at the Tribal Office."

Far away, but growing louder, the deep-throated roar of a 6.2L Supercharged HEMI V8 echoed from somewhere west of Cut Bank.

Trudy shot a glance at Elmer. "Showtime. You sure you don't want to come with me?"

Elmer adjusted his ball cap. "The bigger the lie, the easier it is to believe. Leave your rig parked on the street so he can see it. There should be a pickup in the lot across the street. Little Feet said the keys would be under the floor mat."

"Take care, Brother." Trudy gave Elmer a quick squeeze. "If you get picked up and they question me, I'll swear I was adopted and had no idea my half-brother was such an idiot."

"As soon as it's safe, as soon as I'm able, I'll visit you at your new place in Canada."

"The land of hockey, free healthcare, and Tim Hortons. I'll keep the wood chopped and fireplace stoked."

The unmistakable rumble of a 6.2L engine racing eastward prompted Elmer to step back toward the entrance of the open storage unit. As if on cue, sirens from the south joined the loud chorus. Taking his position just inside and partially concealed by a pallet, Elmer felt a tug of relief—then panic.

In the movies, the hero always had a well-oiled plan, sleek weapons, and perfect hair. Elmer had no weapons, only nasal hair trimmed with tweezers. He couldn't help but think his whole grand plan had the feel of a Looney Tunes episode. Crouching behind a pallet, he imagined himself as Wile E. Coyote holding an ACME detonator, waiting for Road Runner to zoom past so he could blast him to kingdom come.

Then the mental image became all too real. The sound of an explosion reverberated off storage unit doors—but not from Acme TNT. The loud impact came from the front gate, being ripped off its hinges. A white Ford pickup — with busted headlights flashing, grill dented, and a lime-green stripe down the side—screeched to a halt at the far end of Row D.

The Bureau man stepped out.

OLD WEST SHOWDOWN IN ROW D

Monday, March 16, 10:04 a.m.

Elmer shrank back into the shadows, hoping the man from the Bureau of Land Management wouldn't notice the unit's open door.

If Pauly D's guy saw the busted gate and BLM truck parked at the end of Row D, he might assume the worst—that the feds had arrived to arrest Elmer.

"You're a hard man to catch, farmer."

The Bureau man's voice echoed off metal doors, all but funneling his words into the open unit.

"But not a hard man to track. You leave dead germs wherever you go."

Jose Wales, thought Elmer. This guy's thinking he's in the middle of an Old West showdown.

"By the almost unlimited and growing authority vested in me by the United States government, I'm here to bring you in for hoarding vital, scarce disinfectant and cleaning supplies during a national emergency."

Elmer scratched his chin, trying to figure out how to buy time until Paul D's guy arrived. Assuming the mobster stopped. He might just as easily keep driving if he spied a federal agent.

"I know what you're thinking. Did I make six calls or only five? One to local law, one to the county sheriff, then FEMA, DOJ, Centers for Disease Control, and Homeland Security. Truth is, farmer, I lost count in all the commotion. But considering how fast they mobilize for a Lysol-lugging outlaw, you gotta ask yourself one question: Do you feel lucky, old man?"

The sound of hard-sole shoes smacking the pavement grew closer.

"Well, do you?"

Elmer stepped from the storage unit to face the man. "The goods are gone. You're too late."

"That's what they all say … right before they're times up." As if clutching a remote detonator, the Bureau man held up a key fob. "Ever hiked into Glacier National?"

"Can't say as I have. Wanted to, but Dad said we didn't have time."

"There's that word, again."

Looking left, then right to make sure no one lurked in an open unit, he stepped closer.

"The park's beautiful this time of year. Covered in snow, mostly empty of tourists. Wildlife coming out of hiding."

The Bureau man pressed the key fob, causing it to make a chirping sound.

"Not the sort of place you'd want to venture into alone," he continued.

Elmer shifted his gaze to the truck. From the way it rocked and shuddered, he sensed a punch line coming.

"Did you know that, on average, two or three folks die each year?"

Elmer, still watching the truck, shook his head.

"From falls, drownings, exposure. Park officials tell 'em to be careful, but you know how people are—stupid." He stopped two units from where Elmer stood guarding empty Lysol boxes. "Thing is, we don't know how many die each year. Some, maybe a lot, end up as a tasty meal for a pack of wolves or a grizzly or—and this I've witnessed firsthand—a mountain lion. No way to track how many visitors are consumed in the park."

He casually pressed the fob again, and the back window of the camper shell lifted, opening slowly.

"For instance, we had a situation this morning of a mountain lion roaming from the park onto the reservation. You get a big cat like that, you gotta act fast before it kills someone."

The Bureau man kept his gaze steady on Elmer. "I worked with the tribal wildlife guys—offered a little logistical support, helped 'em set traps. Took us a while, but we finally caught the big fella."

He looked over his shoulder at the truck, then back at Elmer.

"You might think one tranquilizer would keep a big cat down for a while."

He eased sideways and stepped into the protection of Elmer's storage unit.

"But once it comes to and gets loose, it'll be one angry critter."

The deep-throated roar of an engine grew louder. At the opposite end of Row D, a Dodge Charger skidded to a stop. Pauly D's guy stepped out, a huge grin spreading across his face.

"Who's this?" the Bureau man asked.

"Owner of the Lysol," Elmer replied.

Pauly D's guy walked to where they stood at the entrance of the unit.

Holding his hand out, he said, "Rocco out of Chicago."

"Like I care," the Bureau man replied.

Pauly D's guy patted the Bureau man on the shoulder, then clamping down, squeezed.

"I think you'll care."

Blood drained from the Bureau man's face.

"Don't you think he'll care?"

"If I were in negotiations with someone in possession of vital cleaning supplies, I'd care," Elmer answered.

Pauly D's guy released his grip: the Bureau man slumped, then rubbed his shoulder.

"Those my boxes?"

Elmer nodded and pulled papers out of the gym bag. "Here's the manifest with my signature verifying you are the rightful owner. There are also receipts and stuff in the bag. You know, for accounting purposes."

Pauly D's guy studied the manifest, then frowned. "Mobster?"

"Didn't have a name to put on the buyer's line," Elmer explained.

"Not a problem, hoss. I've been insulted by lesser men. Some are still alive. What's important is that we all understand who's leaving with these boxes." He handed Elmer the keys to the Charger. "Put those papers on the passenger seat. I'll look them over later."

"Um, see … there's a little problem with you taking these boxes," said the Bureau man. Continuing to massage his shoulder, he asked, "Remind me again your name?"

"Rocco, like Rocky, only with more muscle than Stallone."

"Well, Mr. Rocco, what I mean is, it's sort of my job to make sure that Lysol gets to the people who need it."

Grinning, Pauly D's guy thumped Elmer on the shoulder. "I can see why you invited this joker to our meet. He's good for laughs." His smile fading, he asked, "What people?"

"Well, you know," said the Bureau man, "people who depend on the government for their well-being. Poor people. Old people. People who vote. I work for the government, and if we don't act like we care, my department might lose funding, and I could be out of a job."

"Funny you mentioned a job, because that's almost exactly what my boss said to me. 'Rocco,' he said. 'I need that shipment of Lysol. I've got some hospitals that'll pay top dollar,' he said. 'Get me that shipment and fast or an orderly in one of those hospitals will be tying a tag on your big toe,' he said. Seems to me we both want the same thing for the same reasons—to help folks."

Elmer looked beyond the Bureau man toward the end of the alley where, emerging from the back of the BLM truck, was the largest mountain lion Elmer had ever seen—and over the years, he'd watched a lot of Nature Channel VHS tapes.

"Since this is a matter between you two," Elmer said. "I'll be moseying along."

"Hold on, hoss. You ain't going anywhere until I check to make sure all the goods are here."

Elmer eyed the lift jack, the Bureau man, and the mountain lion standing next to the BLM truck. He needed a plan—preferably one that wasn't bonehead stupid.

Right then a bullhorn blared, "Don't move! This is the Montana Highway Patrol. If you attempt to run, you will be shot!"

Shoving the Bureau man into the alley, Pauly D's guy took cover inside and quickly pulled down the storage unit door.

At the baseball tournament, Elmer's dad had gone out of his way to explain in detail the danger of a Glacier National Park mountain lion.

"Son, they can run up to 50 miles per hour over short distances and have a bite force of around 400 to 500 pounds per square inch. That's enough to grind bone to pulp. Their ability to soar great distances, horizontally up to 40 feet in a single bound, allows them to take down their prey in a single leap. You see one, don't run. You'll never escape if you do."

But Elmer didn't need to outrun the mountain lion. He only had to beat one man. With the big cat sprinting toward its next big meal, Elmer broke into a fast jog.

"Halt! Get down on the ground," blared a trooper's bullhorn.

Two state troopers crouched behind the Charger, one with his gun aimed at Elmer.

"Do not take another …"

A horrific growl echoed through the alley, drowning out the word "step."

Then came the shrill scream of a man, a single gunshot, and silence.

LOOK TO THE SOUTHEAST

Monday, March 16, 10:27 a.m.

Little Feet stepped from a red Mustang and hurried to where Elmer stood on the platform of the Cut Bank train station. "I wasn't sure I'd catch you before you left."

The long blast of a train horn prompted Elmer to look west up the track.

"All the papers and the goods are stored in your warehouse," Elmer said. "Paula D's guy won't be a problem. Least not for a while."

The tribal leader gave a slow nod, but his eyes held a hint of concern. "Double-cross the mob and the feds at the same time? This is a dangerous game you are playing."

Elmer bumped up the bill of his cap. "Yeah, but it's the only play I've got left."

There was a pause, a shared understanding between the two men.

The tribal leader sighed, his voice quieter. "Just make sure you watch your back. Pauly D's people—they do not forget, and they do not forgive."

Elmer eyed the long line of passengers waiting behind the gate to board. "Better you and your people make good use of this than the mob or some government agency.

The clanging of the train's bell followed another long blast from the horn. With diesel engines rumbling, the wheels of Amtrak Train 8 squeaked to a stop.

"If I leave the Lysol to the government, they'll only botch delivering the items to those in need."

"True, my old friend, but I have seen other men killed for less."

Elmer thought about all the times he'd promised Edith that he'd take her to Seattle by train.

"I don't know all of what happened back there at the storage unit with those troopers and that mountain lion, but there's a good chance someone is going home with a toe tag." Elmer adjusted his place in line. "At least it's not me or my sister."

"The fed still may come looking for you."

"I expect they will, but with the receipts and paper trail I left for them in that gym bag, they'll be so busy tracking mob money that I shouldn't be a concern. That's my hope, anyway."

"I have to ask, friend, why go to all this trouble, take such risks, to give us cases of cleaning supplies we can buy ourselves?"

Elmer began, his voice trailing as he fumbled for the right words. "I guess … I guess it's a lot of things stacked together. See, after Edith passed, I made her a promise that I'd try to honor her memory. She was always helping others, taking in strangers who needed a meal. I warned her that one day it would come back to bite her, that one of those vagrants would knock her out cold and rob her blind, but she refused to stop, and those things I worried would happen never did. She was about the most blessed person I know. Good karma, I guess."

"We call it 'Walking in a good way.'"

"I didn't wanna leave this world without doing something she'd be proud of. Felt like I'd spent a lotta years living safe and small. But there's nothing to be gained from that anymore. Especially if the government is going to end up taking what I don't use. Without kids, it goes to the state."

"Not your sister?"

"Being rich would ruin her."

Elmer looked down at his hands, weathered from years of working the land.

"It's not that I feel guilty about what happened to your people. They aren't my problem."

"And still you came all this way," Little Feet replied.

"Taking land is just what folks do. The Nations took from each other, the Conquistadors took from the Native Americans, then Mexico took your land, and the U.S. took more Native American land from Mexico. We might wake up tomorrow and find Russia, China, or North Korea's taken this whole country. Taking is what folks do. But Edith was right—giving makes a body feel better."

"You are a strange breed, Fudd."

"'Extinct,' is what my sister says. And honestly, if that bureau man had asked nicely, I'd have given it to him. But the way he talked left me thinking he'd just take it outright. That got me riled up."

The tribal leader studied Elmer for a moment, then reached into his jacket, pulling out a small bundle wrapped in soft leather.

"Something to remember us by."

Elmer accepted the gift and carefully unwrapped the leather. In his palm lay a beautifully carved sculpture of a baseball player mid-swing, the wood dark and polished.

"You... you made this?" Elmer asked, his voice low with admiration.

"My grandson. He carves miniature totem poles and other items reflecting Native American culture. He's getting rich selling them on the Internet."

"He does all this on the rez?" Elmer asked.

"Upper Manhattan. Smart kid. He sends much of what he earns to our people on the rez."

Elmer ran his fingers over the sculpture, savoring its craftsmanship. "I'll cherish this forever."

The tribal leader placed a hand on his shoulder. "You are a good man, Fudd. If our paths never cross again, I will always remember the moment I first struck you out."

"You got lucky. The ball was off the plate. It should have been a walk and a tie game."

"A win is a win," Little Feet said.

The gate opened and passengers began heading to their cars.

"Chicago by train?"

"Then the Southwest Chief home to Kansas," Elmer replied.

"How fitting."

"Keys are under the floor mat. Give the Charger to someone who'll take care of her. She's a nice ride."

"As is life with friends like you, Fudd."

THE END OF THE BEGINNING

March 14, 7:07 p.m.

From behind Elmer's home and barn, the sun began to set, casting long shadows toward the road.

The train ride home had given Elmer time to think—too much so. Lapsing into an all too familiar melancholy mood, he reflected on how he'd narrowly missed getting arrested, mauled by a mountain lion, and shot by a mobster. His sense of invincibility gone, Elmer's expectation of better days ahead melted away.

Coming down from a mountaintop experience, are we?

Edith—even in the grave, her tender chiding got under his skin. He fixed his gaze on the family's small cemetery plot beneath the front yard's large oak.

"Doing good to others worked for a while. Now I'm just spent."

So? He was beaten down, too, but he got up and went back to helping those too poor and sad to lift their heads.

On the road in front of the house, a black SUV slowed when it neared his drive.

"Guess I expected more."

Like applause? A pat on the back? Joy is for a season, not forever. Get off your duff and go find someone who doesn't have it as good as you.

"I'd rather sit and sulk."

The SUV turned into the drive. Once more, the dread he'd felt the day he met the Bureau man gripped his gut. Government folk on important business drove such a vehicle. So did mobsters.

At your age, he's coming sooner than you think. You better get on with life.

Launching tendrils of dust clouds, the SUV bounced along the rutted drive, pulling to a stop at the corner of the house. The rear passenger door opened and a familiar face emerged.

"Hope you don't mind, but I took the liberty of finding out where you lived."

Jim from Buffalo exited the SUV.

"The way I figure it," Jim continued, "you left me stranded at that motel without so much as a 'kiss my foot,' so you owe me."

Jim pulled a small floral-print overnight bag from the rear passenger seat and waddled toward the house.

"I need a place to do rehab. Your name came to mind."

Elmer bent forward and swept leaves out of an Adirondack chair. "I wouldn't say I'm all that great as a caregiver."

"So long as you don't try to OD me with meds, I'll consider it an upgrade."

The SUV backed up, turned around, and drove away.

"Your son doesn't know you're here, does he?"

"Scottie thinks I'm in Buffalo waiting to get my room back at that death camp."

"Here, let me help you."

Elmer rose and hurried off the porch. Taking Jim's bag, Elmer guided his new house guest up the steps.

Frowning, Elmer adjusted the strap on his shoulder. "What'd you pack? Bricks?"

"Six pack. You know, to celebrate my liberation. Not every rehab patient gets by on kale smoothies and celery juice. And what beer lacks in nutrients my nurse will prescribe when she arrives."

"Nurse?"

"Gretchen. Served in Israel's military," Jim said. "Not an ounce of fat on her. She could snap my neck with her fingers."

"A… nurse?" Elmer repeated. "Here?"

"I could call and tell her to not show, but then you'd be helping with my rehab and I'm not a great patient. Mind if I take a load off?"

"That's why I cleaned off the chair."

Jim eased into the chair.

Pulling a beer from his luggage bag, Jim popped the top. "Here's to hope and a long life."

Elmer took in the sounds of crickets and birds. Far off, a truck downshifted, backfiring.

"I'm not sure I'm going to like this," Elmer said.

"I know I won't," Jim replied. "But what are we going to do? I'm a wild spirit with a new knee that needs time to heal." He took a long chug and belched. "And you're a lost soul looking for love."

"Now, why would you go and say that?"

"An observation is all. And if you say love is overrated, I'll know you're lying. You miss her."

"Now, why go and ruin this gorgeous sunset?"

"Sorry. I'll enjoy this Pabst in silence."

Elmer took a long, slow look at the land, his land, the same patch he'd stood on through storm and drought, through loss and what counted for a quiet, ordinary life.

"I am not looking for love," Elmer said with more force than he intended.

"You say that now, but wait until you meet Gretchen." Jim again reached into his bag. "Beer? It's warm, but at our age, we can't be too choosy."

Elmer had returned to the farm to feel grounded, to be with Edith—and maybe die next to her if he could work it out. Now this: a house guest.

"So tell me," Jim said. "Why'd you do what you did back there?"

"You mean rescuing you?"

"All of it. The Lysol, the tribe on the reservation, that business with Pauly D's guy. Me."

Elmer's mouth twisted into something close to a grin. "You ever make a promise that got under your skin? Deep, I mean, like no matter how many years passed, you'd feel it nagging at you?"

Jim squinted into the dusk. "For me, it's my son. No matter what I do, I always think I could love him better. Just don't know how to show it, I guess."

"Edith made me swear to do something. Didn't make a lot of sense then. But over time, you get to thinking … maybe she was right."

Jim rested his elbow on the armrest and leaned toward Elmer. "So you risked prison and a ball bat to the kneecaps for her."

"Partly. But it's more than that." Elmer reached for the unopened beer atop Jim's bag. "This land here used to be the Nations. And the way I figure it, any little thing I can do to make up for a wrong, even if it's not exactly my fault, is the right thing to do."

Jim raised his beer in a toast. "Well, I'm guessing your wife would be mighty proud of you."

A quiet settled around them. Elmer wasn't sure he'd done enough, not really. But he'd kept his promise to Edith—or close enough to it—and that had to count for something.

"Gretchen?" Elmer asked.

"Gretchen Cohen. Closer to your sister's age than yours, but she's still not bad on the eyes. Guess it's that Middle-Eastern blood."

"Talk much?"

"Nonstop."

"Opinionated?"

"Left the States to serve in the Israeli army? What do you think?"

"I don't think we'll get along, is what I think."

"You see her tomorrow, you tell her that. To her face. That I want to see."

"If I hadn't busted you out of that assisted living place," Elmer said, "would you still be alive?"

"Maybe. Probably not."

"And for that good deed, you bring another woman into Edith's home?" Elmer asked.

"Trust me, you're going to like having her around."

But Elmer wasn't sure about that. Still, as the darkness of dusk settled over his homestead, he felt something he hadn't felt for a long time: hope.

The End

A note from the author:

Edith believed that three things remain forever—hope, faith, and love—and God is the source of all three. For Edith, if there is no God, then where did life come from? In science, there is the law of biogenesis: life comes only from life. Matter does not produce life on its own. So Edith would often ask Elmer, "What is the source of life?" And he'd shrug.

Edith believed God sent His Son to bring all people into a new kingdom where hope, faith, and love expand forever. For Edith, God loves company, and the more, the better. If Jesus was not conceived by the Spirit of God miraculously—as Edith believed—then Mary allowed her own son to suffer and die for something she knew was false.

If Jesus did not rise from the dead—as Edith believed—and the eleven disciples knew His body had been taken, then they suffered beatings, prison, and death for a lie. They gained no power, no wealth, and no safety from living this lie, and watched their families suffer as well.

If God is not love, then where does love come from? If God is who He says He is—love itself—then it follows that He loves you and always has. He offers hope for this life and the life beyond death. That is the hope Elmer wrestles with as he sits on his porch knowing that one day soon, he too, will die. He wants to hope, but will he?

COVID-19 PANDEMIC: TIMELINE AND LASTING IMPACTS (2019–2021)

Timeline of Key Events

December 2019

- First known cases of a novel coronavirus reported in Wuhan, China.

January 2020

- WHO confirms human-to-human transmission.
- First U.S. case confirmed in Washington State.

March 2020

- WHO declares COVID-19 a global pandemic.
- U.S. declares a national emergency.
- Widespread lockdowns begin.

December 2020

- FDA authorizes Pfizer-BioNTech and Moderna vaccines for emergency use.

2021

- Mass vaccination campaigns commence.
- Delta variant leads to a surge in cases.
- Debates over vaccine mandates intensify.

Lasting Changes from the Pandemic

Education

- Remote learning became widespread, impacting student performance and widening the achievement gap.
- Homeschooling and virtual academies saw increased enrollment.
- Students from marginalized communities faced greater challenges due to limited access to technology and resources.

Workplace and Economy

- Shift to remote work in many industries.
- Labor shortages and "The Great Resignation" altered employment trends.
- Supply chain disruptions affected global trade.
- Some remote workers reported declines in social skills and mental health.

Health and Public Behavior

- Increased focus on personal hygiene and public health protocols.
- Widespread use of masks during flu seasons and outbreaks.
- Rise in mental health issues, including anxiety and depression.

Church and Religious Practice

- Many churches moved services online.
- Decline in in-person attendance; some churches did not reopen.
- Religious participation patterns shifted, with some groups experiencing more significant changes.

Politics and Elections

- 2020 election saw record mail-in ballots.
- Polarization over mask mandates, lockdowns, and vaccines intensified political divides.
- Nearly three-quarters of U.S. adults felt the pandemic increased national division.

Technology and Communication

- Video conferencing tools became essential for work, education, and socializing.
- Acceleration in digital services and automation.
- Increased reliance on technology highlighted digital divides.

Mental Health and Society

- Global prevalence of anxiety and depression increased by 25% in the first year of the pandemic.
- Students and young people faced heightened mental health challenges due to isolation and disrupted routines.
- Healthcare workers experienced significant burnout and psychological distress.

Sources and References (APA Style)

U.S. Department of Education, Office for Civil Rights. (2021, June). *Education in a pandemic: The disparate impacts of COVID-19 on America's students.* https://www.ed.gov/sites/ed/files/about/offices/list/ocr/docs/20210608-impacts-of-covid19.pdf

Johnson, A. (2024, December 28). 25% of remote workers' social skills have declined while working from home: Survey. *New York Post.* https://nypost.com/2024/12/28/business/25-of-remote-workers-social-skills-have-declined-while-working-from-home-survey/

World Health Organization. (2022, March 2). *COVID-19 pandemic triggers 25% increase in prevalence of anxiety and depression worldwide.* https://www.who.int/news/item/02-03-2022-covid-19-pandemic-triggers-25-increase-in-prevalence-of-anxiety-and-depression-worldwide

Pew Research Center. (2025, February 12). *How the COVID-19 pandemic affected U.S. religious life.* https://www.pewresearch.org/politics/2025/02/12/how-the-covid-19-pandemic-affected-u-s-religious-life/

Pew Research Center. (2025, February 12). *5 years later: America looks back at the impact of COVID-19.* https://www.pewresearch.org/politics/2025/02/12/5-years-later-america-looks-back-at-the-impact-of-covid-19/

Serrano, M. (2024, January 2). Texas schools are facing a student mental health crisis. *Houston Chronicle.* https://www.houstonchronicle.com/news/houston-texas/education/hisd/article/texas-covid-mental-health-crisis-20205168.php

Margo, N. (2023, December 10). 'Broken': Hidden side effect of COVID-19 leaves health care workers struggling. *News.com.au.* https://www.news.com.au/lifestyle/health/mental-health/broken-hidden-side-effect-of-covid19/news-story/f9cd338a76ab16811772ea7d9a94df7b

www.ingramcontent.com/pod-product-compliance
Lightning Source LLC
Chambersburg PA
CBHW030645190726
48286CB00008B/2672

* 9 7 8 1 9 3 8 4 9 9 3 6 4 *